Love is
a time of enchantment:
in it all days are fair and all fields
green. Youth is blest by it,
old age made benign:
the eyes of love see
roses blooming in December,
and sunshine through rain. Verily
is the time of true-love
a time of enchantment — and
Oh! how eager is woman
to be bewitched!

THE PEACOCK FAN

When Kassim Khan and his wife are killed in an earthquake, their adopted son Dil Bahadur is so devastated he can only think of leaving India and joining his wife and young daughter in England. Before he is able to act on his wish, Dil once more encounters Amara, the beautiful Begum of Jungdah, and feels himself falling for her dangerous charms. Despite Amara's fiercely protective and jealous husband, Ismail Mohammed, the Begum and Dil Bahadur are unable to resist the passion that flares between them, little knowing that their previous sins are about to come home to roost . . .

Books by Katharine Gordon
Published by The House of Ulverscroft:

KATHARINE GORDON

THE
PEACOCK
FAN

Complete and Unabridged

ULVERSCROFT
Leicester

First published in Great Britain in 1996 by
Severn House Publishers Limited
Surrey

First Large Print Edition
published 1997
by arrangement with
Severn House Publishers Limited
Surrey

British Library CIP Data

Gordon, Katharine
    The peacock fan.—Large print ed.—
    Ulverscroft large print series: romance
    1. India—Fiction 2. Love stories
    3. Large type books
    I. Title
    823.9'14 [F]

    ISBN 0–7089–3862–0

Published by
F. A. Thorpe (Publishing) Ltd.
Anstey, Leicestershire
Set by Words & Graphics Ltd.
Anstey, Leicestershire
Printed and bound in Great Britain by
T. J. International Ltd., Padstow, Cornwall

This book is printed on acid-free paper

Prologue

JUNGDAH — country of dreams and nightmares, love and death.

Far in the north of India, Jungdah State is a place of bare mountains and deep valleys, bitterly cold most of the year, a poor place, a scramble of villages built where there is a piece of flat ground and a pocket of soil to cultivate. Each village surrounded by walls, with guarded gates closed at sunset.

The only town, Dhalli, clustered close round the walls of Dhalli Palace, a fortress with high stone ramparts and buildings that had their backs turned to the town, the windows of which faced inwards to the large central courtyard.

A haunted place. Terrible things had happened in Jungdah State, and had left behind a sense of fear that seemed to breathe from the walls of the houses — although, since Ismail Mohammed had come to the State and had eventually succeeded in marrying the widowed

1

daughter of the old Ruler, there had been peace of a sort.

It was a difficult country to rule. A proud people who had been living under the tyranny of a cruel invader looked for quick benefits, instant prosperity and an indulgent ruler. They did not find this. Ismail Mohammed was a soldier, he expected discipline and obedience, and he was avaricious, seeking his own wealth. His wife, the beautiful Begum Amara stood between his uncertain temper and the people of Jungdah. As time passed, only his marriage to her kept his subjects from open rebellion.

Ismail was a disappointed man. He loved his wife deeply, was proud that she had agreed to marry him. He longed for a son to carry on his name. Amara Begum brought him a daughter, born prematurely, seven months after their marriage and then it seemed she was unable to give him another child. His love for his wife overcame his disappointment at first. But as time went on he did not find all that he had hoped for in his marriage. Amara was beautiful, compliant, refused him nothing, appeared to be the perfect wife. But somehow, even in the height of passion, he began to feel that she had escaped him, that he held in his arms only a lovely simulacrum. He began to grow angry and frustrated — and deeply jealous. Who was it in her mind he wondered, making her so distant, even though she responded obediently to all his wishes? He became convinced that there was another man. It could not be her dead first husband — he had been an old man, she could not be dreaming of him. Then who? The question never left him, it tormented him.

The lack of a son added to his unhappiness and his anger. She had borne a son to her dead husband — why not to him, a man in the flower of his life? He took to beating her when he was drunk. His daughter, Yasmin, at first a loving child, drew away from him as she grew to girlhood; she felt his lack of love and his disappointment every time he looked at her. His treatment of her mother terrified her.

Yasmin was fifteen when a visitor to Dhalli Palace remarked on her growing beauty. "You must have found yourself a wife from Kangra, or the Lambagh valley, to have produced such a daughter. All the women of those parts are exceptional. Indeed that daughter of yours reminds me of the women of Lambagh State — from where came the most beautiful of all, dead now, alas. Muna, the dancer, she who married an Englishman. Your girl looks to be as fair as she was."

Muna, the mother of Dil Bahadur. Ismail Mohammed had at last a focus for his jealousy. He questioned Amara fiercely, and she laughed at him. He beat her severely, and she endured the beating, and when she could move, got up and walked away from him, her eyes burning with fury.

But Amara became frightened when she saw how he looked at Yasmin. He would sit and stare at her, saying nothing. Yasmin woke one night and found him bending over her bed, lamp in hand, studying her face, it was his brandy-laden breath that had woken her. She had run screaming to her mother, and thereafter shared her mother's room, and the door was locked against Ismail Mohammed. Amara Begum, unafraid for herself, sent

4

for help to her son Atlar Khan, ruler of the neighbouring State of Pakodi.

Atlar Khan was walking in his garden when he saw the little messenger circling and turning above him. He went at once to his pigeon house, calling to the boy who looked after the birds. As soon as the bird had landed and gone into its house, the boy put his hand in and brought it to Atlar Khan. He took the little palpitating body, and removed the tiny silver cylinder from the clip on its leg. The bird, released, flew up to the platform outside its house, and Atlar Khan removed the scrap of paper from the cylinder and read it. No one but his mother sent him messages by this means, the speediest method she had. He felt a stab of anxiety. He disliked his stepfather very much. The dislike was mutual. He feared for his mother's safety. The note was brief, only asking if he could come on a few days visit. He wondered if she had forgotten that they were all expected to attend the Durbar for the new Ruler of Lambagh's accession. But the last words of the message alarmed him. 'Come soon.'

He decided to leave at once.

He went over the high passes, a hard four days journey. He was sure that there was something wrong in Jungdah. When he arrived in Dhalli Palace, his mother did not come out to welcome him. His sister Yasmin was waiting for him and said he was to come with her to the Zenana. He was surprised to see how she had grown in the year since he had last seen her. "You are a beauty, my sister. You will turn heads in Madore."

"If I am allowed to go."

"Well, of course, we are all going."

"You will hear from our mother."

Amara Begum received him in her chamber. He saw faint bruising, and was ready to go and confront his stepfather, but his mother begged him not to.

"Let be, Atlar my son. He is in an evil humour. I fear that we will not go to the Durbar. I need to leave this place and if he denies us the visit to Madore, I ask you to take us to my sister in Panchghar — but see first if you can persuade him to take us to Madore — for Yasmin's sake."

To Atlar Khan's surprise, he did not

have to do any persuading. Ismail Mohammed suggested at once that he should escort his mother and sister to the Durbar. "I myself will follow later. I have one or two matters of importance to attend to here, and also there is a sale of yearlings in Peshawar that I must visit. It will be of great assistance to me if you will take the women ahead."

There was something in his eyes that worried Atlar Khan. A strange look, lost, questioning. Not like the man. Ismail Mohammed had always been given to terrible outbursts of rage, but this strange look of uncertainty was new. Atlar Khan had the thought that he was perhaps drinking too much — well, he would talk with his mother later. He knew that earlier there had been a bad disagreement between the two over some man Ismail Mohammed favoured as a son-in-law. At present, the best thing that he could do was get his mother and sister away from Jungdah.

Three days later they left, and Ismail Mohammed watched them go, and then retired to talk to his chief minister as to his ordering of the State in Ismail

Mohammed's absence. He also planned over a drink how he would find out, once and for all, if Amara Begum had been unfaithful to him.

He left for Madore three days after the others. He did not go to Peshawar. He did not want to leave his wife unwatched too long in Madore.

1

THE city of Madore lay silent under the burden of the summer heat.

Nothing moved in the streets, no voices called. The windows of the houses were shuttered, the doors showed blank faces to the sun. Nothing moved in the houses, the feeling of sleep filled the midday silence. Even the pigeons who lived on the roof tops were still, stunned by the sun that had taken all the colour from a sky seemingly made of iron, hanging over the city, forcing the heat down into the narrow streets.

Slowly the day burned away and at last the heat began to lessen. The sun was low on the horizon as two riders and a long train of retainers entered the city and rode slowly through the streets. Their coming raised echoes from the walls of the houses. Dogs, lying comatose in the shadow of the walls, woke to run yapping at the horses; pigeons, disturbed, rose

9

with a clap of wings into the evening sky. As at a signal, the first shutters were flung back, shopkeepers were roused — the city was awake.

* * *

The two tall men leading the cavalcade were known to everyone in Madore city. Dil Bahadur, commander of the Lambagh State forces, and his son, Jamshyd Khan were popular and respected. There were greetings called to them, women hidden behind the screening shutters peered out and sighed and smiled to see the return of these two men, who, apart from being good to look upon, represented security and honest rule for the city. Madore was close to the border between British India and the Hill States. Beyond the city walls lay the desert, a no man's land, where lawlessness ruled, and men attacked the city at will, until the rulers of Lambagh drove them away and brought peace to the area. Indeed, the Lambagh family were loved and honoured in Madore, and the death of the late ruler, Kassim Khan, had brought grief and dismay to the whole district. Kassim Khan and his wife had gone to the city of Dharmasala, at the top of the Kangra valley, to attend a festival there. A terrible earthquake had devastated the area, and among the many hundreds killed had been the ruler of Lambagh and his wife Sara Begum.

The two men, riding past with their entourage on the last leg of their long journey from the hills were, the citizens of Madore knew, the first of many. There was to be a great Durbar to celebrate the occasion of Jiwan Khan's accession to the Guddee of the three states, Lambagh, Jindbagh and Diwarbagh, which formed the State of Lambagh. Rulers of mountain states throughout the area would be coming with their families to pay their respects to the greatest of them all — the new Ruler of Lambagh, Jiwan Khan, only son of Kassim Khan. The celebrations would last for days, and bring much honour and prosperity to the city of Madore.

The thought of the festivities, the princes who were coming to stay in the city, and the wealth that would come to Madore, had healed much of the grief

11

that six months before had devastated the Lambagh Valley and the cities that stood on the borders between British India and the lands of the native states. Kassim Khan had ruled the valley for so long. Jiwan Khan was well known to all, but seemed young to have inherited the throne — and he had no son. The heir was still Dil Bahadur, whose English birth was long forgotten. All that was remembered of his past life was that he was a successful leader of the states forces, and the son of the beautiful Muna, the Rose of Madore. No one believed for a moment that his father had not been Kassim Khan.

His son, James, known in Lambagh and every other part of the north as Jamshyd Khan, acknowledged the greetings that were shouted to them as they rode through the streets, but Dil Bahadur seemed lost in thought, and looked serious, almost grim, and some men in the passing crowd looked at each other and wondered if there had been trouble in the hills. Finally, an old man of some authority questioned the leader of the retinue. The man, tired by the long journey, was short in his answer.

"He grieves for his father. What else? It is only six months. Dil Bahadur does not forget so easily the father he loved — they were closer than father and son, thinking alike. What trouble should there be in our hills? The trouble builds down here, where this heat breeds riots as well as brain fever." The questioner, rebuked, but satisfied, stepped back, and passed on the news that there was nothing to be anxious about — nothing but mourning troubled the Lord Dil Bahadur.

If Dil Bahadur had not been thinking of the past, of all the many times he had ridden through Lambagh with Kassim Khan beside him, if grief had not clouded his mind, he would have seen and recognised the man who came from a shuttered house to stand in the shadows to watch the cavalcade go by. Dil Bahadur had a noticing eye and he would certainly have remarked on the way the man stared with neither friendship nor pleasure on his face.

As Dil Bahadur rode by, the man turned to look after him and his teeth showed in a smile that was more like a snarl. He was a man of substance, tall, handsome, and well dressed. Two uniformed men, their turbans burning yellow and orange in the hot sun, stood behind him, while two more led up horses from the narrow alleyway that ran down from the main street.

The watching man waited until Dil Bahadur and Jamshyd had passed before he mounted his horse. As he settled himself in the saddle, he said, over his shoulder, "That is the one. The elder of the two. Have watchers put on him — and on the younger man too. Day and night, everywhere they go — and every evening I want news of them and their movements. Every evening after sunset."

There was no one to hear this exchange, no one noticed the strange, considering look of hatred on the face of this watcher, as he stared after the Lambagh party before he turned his horse away.

As Dil Bahadur and Jamshyd rode through the streets they left the commercial part of the city behind, and entered tree-lined streets, where high walls hid large houses, some large enough to be known as mahals, palaces. These were the town residences of the Hill Rulers and the bustle that was going on around these places spoke of imminent arrivals. It was necessary for the pair to slow their progress to avoid the various horsemen and coolies who were unloading baggage outside one tall iron gate. Jamshyd saw an open carriage waiting to enter, and his eye was caught by a splash of blazing colour.

Seated in the carriage were two women, one heavily veiled, the second a young girl who had pushed back her veil and was fanning herself. The fan was a silver handled peacock feather fan, which she was handling with skill, giving herself and the woman next to her the benefit of whatever cool the fan could bring. The outriders and the driver of this carriage wore brilliant orange turbans. The whole equipage gave a patch of rich colour to the dusty road where they waited, pleasing to the eye of the young man, who almost drew rein to look at them, and then, as the outriders turned to stare at him, recollected himself and rode on after his father. It was not at all suitable to be caught staring at the womenfolk of a hill Raja, however harmless was your interest. It was the colour, and the graceful movement of the girl with the peacock fan, that had caught his eye. He wondered who they could be, and when he caught up with his father would have asked him, but saw that he was lost in some reverie that had brought him no pleasure. He looked to be full of sorrow, and Jamshyd knew that he was, and knew what caused it.

It was six months now since the death of Kassim and his wife Sara, but Dil Bahadur showed no signs of getting over his grief. Jamshyd felt his usual painful anger whenever he saw his beloved father distressed. If only his mother would come back or, failing that, write to his father and set him free to make another life for himself. There did not seem to the young man much hope of his mother ever returning to India. Her hatred of the country had grown out of all proportion, and had conquered her longing to be with her husband.

Now she appeared to have settled in England and for months — over a year now — there had been no letter from her saying that she was returning. Only letters demanding that he and his father return to England to live. This was ridiculous to Jamshyd, who had never imagined that he would spend his life — once he grew up and had the right to choose — anywhere else but here, in the northern hill states of this beloved country of his birth.

As for his father, his life was here also. There had been no question of his going back to take up his life as a country gentleman on his estates in leafy Kent. At least, there had not been any idea of this happening — until the tragedy of Dharmasala had robbed Dil Bahadur of his dearest friend, his beloved adopted father, Kassim Khan. Now he spoke openly of Jamshyd's return to England, and Jamshyd was unhappy, not only at the thought of his father leaving him, but more, of the unhappiness that he was sure would come to Dil Bahadur, without the life he knew, and his friendships here in India.

To all intents, Dil Bahadur was one of the Lambagh family — and the heir to the throne of the Valley States should anything happen to Jiwan Khan, who was childless. Jamshyd, who loved his father, and had taken the trouble to get to know him, was certain there was no happiness waiting for Dil Bahadur in England. The life of a country gentleman — the long, dreary winters — his mother's demanding social life — was his father to fill his days with things of this trivial nature? Dil Bahadur, the great soldier of the north, a man held in respect from one end of the northern valleys to the southern seas of the Malabar coasts? Impossible.

Jamshyd spent his days in argument with Dil Bahadur, and now, when he began "my father — " Dil Bahadur turned with a smile, and said, "Jamshyd. I beg you. No more argument. I have made no decision yet, and I cannot bear any more discussion on this subject. You are right in everything you say — only, son of my heart, say no more now. I am deaf with your reasoned arguments — let be now."

"No. I have no intention of saying

anything further. You are a grown man, you know your own mind, and I do not intend to say anything more."

"Thank you, Jamshyd. I am relieved to hear this, I had begun to feel that you saw me as a small and senseless child."

"I was only going to ask you who, among the Hill Rulers, has the livery of orange and yellow turbans and a gold crescent as a badge. We have just ridden past their house, I think."

Orange turbans, a gold crescent. The slow even rhythm of Dil Bahadur's heart altered its beat a fraction, but his voice was steady as he replied.

"That sounds like the livery of Jungdah. But they have no town residence here. They must have taken one for the duration of the Durbar — it is unusual, Ismail Mohammed seldom leaves his State — except to buy horses."

"Well, if that was Mohammed he has brought his family down with him, and from the amount of baggage they had, I should say he intends a long stay. Jungdah — is that not the state where you fought a great battle and finally defeated the despised Sagpur — and killed him? I look forward to meeting the Jungdah people."

Dil Bahadur did not answer his son. He took a fold of his turban and pulled it across his face. They were leaving the city by the north gate and the dust of the desert was rising about them. Ten miles outside the city lay their destination, the Madore Palace, the home of many generations of the Lambagh family whenever they came down from their mountain valleys to visit the city.

The Madore Mahal slept behind high red walls. The gardens were green, the lawns carefully watered, the tall trees with their pools of dark shade creating an illusion of coolness in the dusty plain that lay outside the walls. The palace had been silent and empty since the death of Kassim and Sara. Now the servants had been working to bring life to at least one wing of the enormous, sprawling building. The rest of the old palace was shuttered and silent, the servants waiting to be told how many visitors were coming. Jiwan Khan, the ruler, and his wife Roshanara would have the centre wing, the rooms where the ruler and his wife always stayed. But their servants had not yet arrived; the rooms were left as they had been when Sara had last stayed in them. The servants who lived in the quarters behind the palace had not entered those rooms. They spoke, of course, of voices heard at night, of footsteps, where no person walked, of music sounding softly in empty rooms. They would not enter to disturb the spirits returned to a place they loved.

The sun had gone, the sky was streaked with brilliant colour which faded very quickly into the shadows of the evening. Birds were loud in the trees, settling for the night. Their voices slowly grew quieter as the sky grew dark, and at last the waiting servants heard the sound they were waiting for, the sound of horses coming fast along the road outside the red walls.

As they dismounted, and threw their reins to the waiting syces, Jamshyd glanced at his father. It must be hard for him to come here, where so often before Kassim would have been standing on the steps to welcome him, and his wife

Laura would be waiting in the women's quarters to fling herself into her husband's arms. There had never been any doubt in Jamshyd's mind of his mother's love for Dil Bahadur. So why was she so adamant about never returning to India?

He found it in his heart to dislike his beautiful mother, who appeared to think of no one but herself. He was relieved to see a figure descending the steps, here at least was an old friend to take some of the emptiness away from this sad arrival.

"Rabindra! How long have you been here, what good fortune to see you!" Dil Bahadur greeted the man who had served him for eight years.

The two men embraced, and Rabindra, with his hand still holding Dil Bahadur's arm, turned smiling to Jamshyd.

"The tiger and the tiger's cub! Where else would I be but here when there is such an arrival! I came down through the Zogi La, and over the Bara Lacha to greet you. I wish you had been with me, it was a grand march — and I have plenty of news for the Commander of the State Force — aha! See the old tiger's eyes blaze with interest — wait till I tell you what I heard and saw — but it is more for laughter than action."

Jamshyd's heart warmed as usual to see this man, one of his father's closest friends, Rabindra, the free spirit, who wandered the length of the continent, always returning with news and quite often the results of the news were frontier troubles, small battles between hill states — and always to the advantage of Lambagh. Tall, slender, ageless, there were strange stories told about this man, but to Jamshyd he was one of the most interesting men of his father's circle — if anyone could persuade Dil Bahadur to give up foolish plans to leave his valleys, Rabindra was the man.

The dust of the roads bathed away and forgotten, the three friends now sat on the chibutra, the wide marble square that jutted out over the garden, food and drink on a low table before them, and at least the youngest member of the party looked forward to an evening of interesting and amusing talk.

Jamshyd was relieved to see that already, with Rabindra's coming, his father looked less sad and worried. This man's stories of his travels and of people he had met, ranged from the horse dealing State of Kathiawar to the waterless deserts of Sind and up to Baluchistan and from there to the foothills of the Himalayas and their own mountains and beyond. He spoke of horse sales, where splendid animals were put on display, of fighting camels and smuggled gold, of dancing girls of fantastic beauty walking barefaced through the bazaars of Quetta and Kandahar, and the camel caravans that travelled the old silk routes, until Jamshyd was wild with envy.

"I need some leave. Father, when Rabindra next goes off on his travels, I would like to go with him. Rabindra, please, it would be good for me. When do you think you will go again?" Rabindra turned to him, smiling.

"Indeed, it would give me pleasure to have your company. How you have changed in this last few years! I see no young James, the English boy with two names, now. You are entirely Jamshyd, and a son of the valleys, in spite of your blue eyes. What do you think, Dil

Bahadur? May I borrow the tiger cub for a month or two?"

Dil Bahadur's thoughts were far away, the words 'the boy with two names' had taken his mind back to the arguments he had had with Laura, his wife, who was so determined that their son remain 'English' in every way, live permanently in England, safely kept from Indian influences. How angry she had been when he had gently reminded her that the boy was the grandson of Muna, and that he was as much Muna's grandson as he was the grandson of her father Sir Edward Addison. The arguments had finally settled when James was eighteen. He had decided what he wished to do, had travelled out to India and with his father's glad permission had joined the Lambagh State Forces — and was no longer the boy of two names. Laura had been bitterly hurt, and it had been then that she had stopped returning on periodic visits to India.

Now, as Rabindra repeated his question, he turned smiling to Jamshyd. "If that is what you would like to do with your next leave, boy, I think it good — you will learn much — and could not have a better teacher."

"I shall guard him with my life — and he will no doubt guard me and be company for me. It is lonely work sometimes, in strange places, and I grow older."

Dil Bahadur laughed at him. "Not too old, apparently, to come down over the Zogi La pass. That is a far cry from the street of Baluchistan. What rumour took you up there?"

"The rumour of the snows. I was sick of dust and crowds and needed the silence of those high mountains. I had company for the last ten days. I came up with young Atlar Khan of Pakodi on his way down here. He was escorting his mother and his sister. Ismail Mohammed comes later, he had some dispute to settle in Jungdah. It seems there is always trouble in that state. Ismail Mohammed is not the most patient of rulers. I heard that the Panchayat are inclined to speak more freely with the Begum Amara, which is natural — she is the daughter of the old ruler, and blood speaks. But they will have to settle their trouble this time without her calming hand — she has come down for the Durbar with her child Yasmin."

Dil Bahadur had not heard a word that Rabindra had said after the mention of the Begum Amara. How that woman haunted him! He had thought himself single-hearted in his love for his wife, had struggled to put the heat and passion that had filled his days in Jungdah away, firm in his devotion to Laura, no matter what she did, she was his wife — and yet — the mere mention of Amara's name had stirred his blood. So strange, so sweet, the Begum of Jungdah had been. Amara, part of his youth. What could she be like now, married to Ismail Mohammed, and mother of a child. Sixteen years had passed since he had said his farewells to Amara, and the parting had left a scar.

Through a haze of memories he said, "Yasmin? Is that the daughter's name? A girl for Ismail Mohammed. He won't have liked that. He wanted an heir. The child is what age now? Ten, twelve?" Rabindra's eyes studied his face.

"Nay, Dil Bahadur. She is approaching

sixteen — born early after their marriage — a seven month's child. It is said up there that the Begum was wilful, would not rest, continued to ride too long, and as a result had a seven month's child. But a fine child, healthy, and with all her mother's charms. She will be a great beauty when she is grown. A rose in bud at present."

A rose in bud thought Jamshyd. That girl I saw with the peacock feather fan! That must be the girl of whom they speak. It must be her. A rose in bud? No. The description was not right. She seemed to him, thinking back, to match her name. Jasmin blossom, white, delicate and charming.

The moon was high, filling the garden with silver light. There was jasmin growing nearby; he could smell the gentle nostalgic perfume. The wine he had enjoyed and had swallowed thirstily, ran in his veins like fire. Yasmin — a suitable name for a girl like the girl he had seen, a silver name — a silver night in which to dream — even his father looked to be dreaming. Thinking of my mother, thought James, my mother, who does not think of him.

The moonlight was so bright, too bright to hide dreams, and Rabindra's eyes were too interested, shifting from Dil Bahadur's face to Jamshyd's dreaming eyes. Dil Bahadur did not notice, but Jamshyd came out of his reveries to see the amused, interested eyes studying him, and felt that under that gaze, all his thoughts were laid bare for Rabindra to know. He moved, stood up and made a business of lighting a cigar, and Rabindra, watching him, suddenly laughed and said, "The tiger's dream — and even I feel dreams at the edge of my mind. It is not only the moon working magic, it is that we are all three exhausted. I came up from Safed today — when did you two leave Faridkote? This morning? Let us for pity's sake go to our beds. The next few weeks will be full of excitement of one kind and another. We will need all our wits and our strength. Throw your cigar away boy! You are asleep on your feet."

Rabindra was right. Jamshyd was asleep moments after he had thrown off his clothes and lain down on his bed. Deep, heavy sleep, moonlight and dreams forgotten.

Rabindra did not try to sleep. He had too many things to think about, too many dangers for Dil Bahadur and his son crowded his mind. He lay thinking and it was daylight before he slept.

It was late into the night when Dil Bahadur gave up tossing on his bed and finally rose and went to stand on the balcony outside his room. The night air was cool, there was a divan there, he would stretch out on that and try for sleep in the night breeze.

The moon was not his friend. Full moon, round as a silver coin, poured down its light. The whole garden was laid out before him, clearly marked in black and white, shadow and silver.

By some strange alchemy, the place was altered to his sight. The balcony seemed higher, suspended in air above a paved court. The surrounding wings of the old Madore Mahal were the high walls of another place. There was a silence so intense that it became a dream silence; no real night could be so quiet. Not a breath of air now, not a whisper of a moving leaf, nothing but the breathing of the night, imagined, not heard, and the faint reminiscent scent of jasmin flowers and white roses, roses that were growing at another time, in a different place.

Against his will Dil Bahadur was snatched back to a place he had avoided, even in thought, for over sixteen years. Jungdah.

Jungdah as it had been when he had last seen it. Held under a curfew that lasted from sunset to noon. No sound or movement from the village, gripped and terrorised, silent, breathing fear.

Why should he think of Jungdah now, on this moon-enchanted night? What had Rabindra released in his mind, by casually speaking of the Begum of Jungdah? Amara! For a moment Dil Bahadur thought he had called her name aloud, and expected to see her standing before him. No. He was alone. Only a disturbed bird called out suddenly, breaking the white silence of the night.

Dil Bahadur turned and went blindly back into his room and closed the shutters against the intrusive moon. He lay on his bed and tried for sanity, telling himself he had been alone and without love for too long. At last he fell into an exhausted sleep.

In the morning he was rested. He reminded himself that Jamshyd was with him, he had friends, he had plenty to do, he had a life he knew. If he was lonely for Laura, there was nothing he could do about that except endure. She was his wife, she might remember this and return. If she did, he wondered again, how he would receive her? This time she had gone in anger, and left him angered too. Had time healed the hurt? While he was wondering how long it took to heal such wounds of the heart, he heard Rabindra and Jamshyd going to the veranda to break their fast, and was glad to go out and join them, and hear their plans for the day.

Of Amara he did not allow himself to think. The momentary madness of the night before was over, leaving behind it, like the scent of dried rose petals, only the feeling that once there had been roses.

Jamshyd expected his father to speak

about the family from Jungdah, and perhaps suggest calling on them. This did not happen. He looked towards Rabindra. Perhaps he would mention them. But Rabindra was studying his father, and Jamshyd saw that Dil Bahadur seemed depressed and tired. Even the arrival of his old friends from Jungdah had not lifted his sorrow. But surely he must want to see them? They were close friends, were they not? Atlar Khan, Ruler of Pakodi, had been at school with Jamshyd, and they had become as close as brothers. He had spoken of Dil Bahadur as if he was a god. The stories of how Dil Bahadur had come to the rescue of the family of the ruler of Jungdah and almost lost his life, of the brilliantly conceived battle he had fought and won to free the people of Jungdah from the tyranny of an enemy ruler, of how he had killed that enemy . . . Atlar Khan said that Dil Bahadur was worshipped in Jungdah. "On feast days they bring flowers and ritual gifts to place beneath his portrait. You are so lucky, Jamshyd, to be the son of such a man. I used to pretend that I was his son, that he had adopted me because my father was dead. Dil Bahadur was a great friend of my real father you know, Ali of Pakodi gave him a sword and a horse when he first came from England. A man to admire and love."

All that love and admiration yet his father had never mentioned that he knew Ali of Pakodi, Atlar Khan's dead father. Now it seemed that he was in no hurry to call on the family. And Rabindra? Surely Rabindra would call on them — and I, thought Jamshyd, I could go with him — but Rabindra was apparently going to ride out twenty or so miles to meet Jiwan Khan and ride back with his entourage. He suggested that Jamshyd might like to come with him, but Jamshyd shook his head.

"Jiwan Khan will see enough of me for the next few weeks. I must go and see Atlar Khan, and talk of what we have to do — we have not had our orders yet."

After Rabindra had left them, Jamshyd turned to his father, seeing his shadowed eyes and the marks of sorrow that were making him seem suddenly old. Dil Bahadur old! Impossible.

"Father, did you sleep at all last

night?" He had to repeat his question, and when he did Dil Bahadur was testy.

"Of course I slept! Jamshyd my son, I hope you are not going to try and play nursemaid to me for the rest of our lives? I slept, I am eating, I am well. I have a great deal to think about, this Durbar is going to take all our wits, as Rabindra said last night. Do you realise that there will be twenty rulers in Madore for two weeks? Better if you stop thinking of me, and think about what you are going to have as duties. There are three of you on duty all the time, am I right?"

Jamshyd! He remembered how angry his mother was when the Lambagh family gave him his Indian name — his father had always tried not to use it in her presence — and now he used it more often than not. Perhaps he was resigning himself, perhaps his mother would never come back. Indeed it might be better if she didn't, he was sure that it was thoughts of her that was making his father so difficult to live with.

"There are three of us, yes. Atlar Khan of Pakodi, Sadik of Chikor, and myself. I think we will have, as you say, plenty to do. These princes are so jealous of precedent."

Dil Bahadur was frowning.

"Did you say Atlar Khan was one of the A.D.C.s? A strange choice, he comes from such a distance. I would have thought young Dewa of Jindbagh was a better choice, after all, his state is part of Lambagh."

"Young Dewa broke his leg playing polo, and although he is of course coming to Madore, he will not be doing very much. Jiwan Khan gave me the choice and I chose my companions. Atlar Khan was at school with me, father, you remember, and he is like a brother to me, and Sadik is a friend also."

Dil Bahadur looked at his son in silence. Atlar Khan a brother — for God's sake, was the boy telling him that he had heard scandal, that he had guessed? No. There was no sign of anything but pleasure in Jamshyd's face. He studied his son, trying to see him as a stranger might. The young tanned face was handsome enough, blue eyes, dark hair falling over his forehead — certainly there was no

36

likeness between Jamshyd and Atlar Khan. In fact, Jamshyd resembled his English great grandfather more than he did his father. Dil Bahadur remembered his grandfather well, and thought how pleased he would be with this splendid young man.

But Atlar Khan — the last time Dil Bahadur had seen him, it had shaken him. Now, every time he shaved he was reminded of the young ruler of Pakodi State. Was it his conscience making him see a likeness where none existed? Or *did* the boy resemble him, was he in truth the fruit of one night's passion in Bombay? No one had ever remarked on a likeness, but he had been careful to avoid the boy and, perhaps, now that he was a man, the likeness would be less. There had never been a whisper of scandal. There must never be. He would avoid as many of the coming festivities as he could. Jiwan Khan would understand, and everyone else would put it down to the fact that he was still mourning the death of Kassim Khan.

Jamshyd moved restlessly, and Dil Bahadur realised that he was still staring blankly at his son. He looked away, and said, "I am glad that you will be working with your friends. You will have little free time, I fear — Jiwan Khan will have to visit most of the rulers, and you will be with him of course quite apart from the meetings that Jiwan Khan will hold himself. I do not envy you, and I think you will be glad to return to regimental duties when this is over. You are seeing Atlar Khan this morning? Please give him my greetings. Jamshyd, think no more of me, I have plenty to do. Go and enjoy your last day and night of freedom for some time to come." He was smiling as he waved his son away, but the smile did not reach his eyes and Jamshyd went away feeling angry with his mother. She should be here — or she should write and say she was not returning, and set his father free.

He rode past the iron gates where he had seen a brougham waiting with the girl with the peacock fan — the young daughter of Ismail Mohammed. It *must* be her that Rabindra had spoken of the night before. The veiled woman in the carriage must have been the beautiful Begum Amara. He felt he had glimpsed a legend and longed to see more, but the gates were closed and two mounted sentries sat on their horses, watching him ride by. Men of Jungdah with expressionless faces; he felt their slanted eyes move to watch him pass.

He came to the maidan that lay between the walled city and the Madore Mahal and gave his impatient horse rein, and enjoyed the freedom of a good gallop. Ahead he could see the walls of the city, and reined in to enter the gates, riding slowly for at this time the streets were teeming with people going about their business before the heat of the day became too great.

The Pakodi Ghar was hidden behind a thick belt of trees, and already the shade was welcome, although it was still early. The guard at the gate stood back salaaming, and he rode through, and up the long drive that led to the house. He saw gardeners working among the flower beds, and envied Pakodi having his own place. It was time he had somewhere of his own too, but how could he leave his father? It was becoming something he would have to give very serious thought to.

There were four horses waiting beside the steps of the old Pakodi Palace. Horses, and two uniformed servitors. Jamshyd was delighted when he saw the orange turbans pinned with a gold crescent. They were old men, tall and upright, hill men, respectable servants, and the horses were splendid animals. Four horses — who had ridden over to see Atlar Khan from the house with the mounted sentries and the barred gate?

As he dismounted, a syce came running to take his horse. A house servant was already coming down the steps to greet him.

"The Nawab Sahib is here?" Jamshyd asked.

"Heaven born, he walks in the garden over there. If it would please you to enter and sit, I will send to tell him."

"No thank you. No need. I will go and join him — I know my way." Jamshyd knew the garden well. He walked across the lawns with their blazing flower beds and entered the deep shade of the trees that sheltered the more private part of the garden. Here the air was cooled by man-made streams and fountains, and sitting in a small marble pavilion, Jamshyd saw Atlar Khan with another man and a girl.

The girl with the peacock fan.

Atlar Khan came of the pavilion to meet him, laughing with pleasure, and the two men embraced.

"Ho, brother of my heart! It has been too long — I would have come today, but as you see I have guests myself — and tomorrow we will be stuffed into hot uniforms doing our duty — which is what? I have no idea why I have been honoured by this appointment."

"And I have no idea why I am honoured either — but I have my suspicions."

The handsome man who had come to join them was the heir to the very rich State of Chikor. He had also been to school in England with the other two, and had gone to the Military Academy with them, and was the third member of a close and valuable friendship. As he embraced Sadik, Jamshyd said, "Suspicions? Are you suggesting some

41

plot, Sadik Bhaiya?"

"Yes. I am asking myself why your Uncle has asked for me to serve him during this time of festival. I do not need to ask, I see quite clearly why. You have to take up this duty for family reasons, therefore you have ensured that neither of your close friends will be free to enjoy the Durbar, because you cannot. True or false?"

"Perfectly true." Jamshyd ducked away from the hand that struck at him. "Are you not my brothers, therefore you are also family members of the Lambagh Ruler. He so regards you, anyway. He gave me my choice, you should be honoured. But your manners were always poor, Sadik. Look now, you have a lady sitting alone, and are attempting to start a brawl — Jiwan is not my Uncle — as you very well know." Atlar Khan intervened.

"Come you two! Jamshyd, you have not met my sister." He led the way to the little pavilion, embowered in flowering creepers, where the girl was sitting.

She was small and slender, smaller than he had thought, and seemed very young. She was looking down as they came up to her, he saw the half circles of thick dark lashes, matching curved eyebrows, the dark shining hair. She was dressed in white, the long shirt and full trousers of the northern women. She looked up when Atlar Khan said her name, and her wide, pale grey eyes looked straight at Jamshyd.

He knew her. He had known her all his life. Seen her in dreams, both waking dreams and the long confused dreams of the night. Sweet unknown, and known — who are you, where have you come from? He stared at her, and saw the flush that coloured her cheeks as she turned her head away, looking down at the fan she held. Four peacock feathers in a chased silver holder.

Atlar Khan completed his introduction, Jamshyd murmured something polite, he never knew later what he had said. She put her hands together, palm to palm, and raised them to her forehead in the customary form of greeting. The fan slipped from her lap and fell, and Jamshyd bent and picked it up and handed it to her. As she took it, their hands touched and he felt the spark of that touch run through his whole body, and stepped back as if he had indeed been burned.

Time passed in a kind of mental blur for Jamshyd. It seemed that they were about to ride down the river road, to the ford, and cross there to spend the first part of the morning eating a picnic lunch in the Pila Ghar, an old house that stood on the banks of the river. Then they were taking a boat down the river to catch the best of the breeze in the hot afternoon. Yasmin was sent back to the house to see to the servants and make sure that they had a suitable picnic prepared. When the men were alone, Atlar Khan apologised for what must seem a childish outing.

"Forgive me — but this is a pleasure for the girl. She has spent all her life in Jungdah, shut up with her mother, her grandmother and old servants. This is her first visit to a city of any size, and I want to do as much for her as I can. She is almost sixteen, and before she knows it she will be married and shut up in her husband's Zenana — I tell you, if she wasn't my half-sister, I would offer

44

for her myself, just to save her. Some of these hill rulers round Jungdah are not what I would choose for her. My mother is, of course, fighting against the man chosen by Ismail Mohammed — a married man of fifty, rich and one to whom Ismail owes favours as well as money. Yasmin knows nothing of the battle that is being fought on her behalf, but I am afraid for her. The man is rich, and Ismail Mohammed is mercenary, and possessive of his wife. If Yasmin had been a boy — well, my mother would have had more power. As it is — one girl child in fifteen years — she has no say in anything very much now. He is angered all the time that she bore a son to my father and not for him. He never forgets that there was a chance for him to rule in Pakodi, until my posthumous birth put him out of the running. My mother adores her daughter and will fight hard for her happiness — meantime, I am going to give Yasmin as much pleasure as I can. I am fortunate to be allowed to have her out like this unchaperoned — and I must get her back before sunset — I promised."

"How strange it is that mothers always imagine that anything that could happen to a girl will happen after dark," said Sadik. "Surely the hours of daylight could be as sweet as the dark hours — and I can imagine that things could easily happen to one as beautiful as your sister, night or day — those eyes would bring light to the darkest hours — and pleasure to the sunlight."

"Well, turn your eyes aside, brother. Nothing is going to happen to Yasmin. As for you, possess your lustful soul in patience until the dark hours of tonight. This very night I am going to entertain you both at the House of Pomegranates. Among other delights they produce very good food."

"And other delights?" asked Sadik.

"Certainly other delights. The night may well be as long and as sweet as you would wish."

Jamshyd was silent. He knew the House of Pomegranates well, not only because it had once belonged to his grandmother, Muna, the beautiful dancer of Madore. Now the house was one of the oldest and best of the houses of pleasure in the street which was called the street of the harlots.

"I have heard of the new girl there," said Atlar Khan. "A girl who dances with her whole body — a girl from Turkey. Very beautiful, they say, and very charming. I have booked her for the night. And the famous Lara is there of course."

"Who is Lara?"

"Wait and you will see. Wait until tonight. Hush now, here comes Yasmin."

Jamshyd turned to watch Yasmin walking towards them. He thought that she did not walk, she floated, the morning breeze blowing her silks about her. The Turkish dancer, and Lara the beautiful entertainer — what were they? Here was the freshness of the morning walking towards them, he had no thoughts of the night.

2

THE heat of the day was mounting as they rode out of the gates of Pakodi Mahal and turned for the river road.

The road ran alongside the river, and was lined with thick-trunked, dark-leaved, mango trees. The river was wide and flowed quietly, there was barely a ripple to disturb its surface, but the air was cooled by the light breeze off the water. Yasmin had veiled herself, only her eyes showed. The dark shade threw green shadows on her white clothes, and caught emerald glints in her eyes as she turned to look at Jamshyd, who rode on one side of her, with Sadik riding on the other. Atlar Khan led the way, and set the pace. Jamshyd saw that Yasmin was an excellent rider, she rode astride like a boy, and indeed, with her loose shirt and trousers hiding her figure, she could have been a youth, riding out with friends. Presently Atlar Khan let his horse go, and the others followed. The horses were fresh and enjoyed the gallop. When they pulled up at the ford, Yasmin's veil had fallen round her throat and her hair was loose on her shoulders. Jamshyd saw Sadik look at her, and look again, with a warm interest, complimenting her on her riding, and for the first time in his life knew the burn of jealousy.

Atlar Khan had sent servants ahead with rugs and cushions, food and drink. The old house was cool and welcoming. Looking round, Atlar Khan said, "Jamshyd, does this house not belong to you? I heard that when Kassim Khan came to be ruler, he gave this house to your grandmother Muna, who had helped to save Kassim and Sara when they were fleeing from Hardyal, that enemy of the Lambagh Family."

"Yes — it belongs to my family, like the House of Paradise in Faridkote — Kassim Khan was generous to my family."

Atlar Khan laughed. "Your family have served Lambagh well — in any case, your father is still the heir. Jiwan Khan is

49

childless. A sad thing it would be if your father was not the heir — it would give the government the opportunity to insist on choosing their own man to rule Lambagh, may Allah the merciful forbid such a thing!"

"Why does Jiwan Khan not take a second wife, since this one is barren?" Sadik spoke casually, looking at Jamshyd, and did not see Atlar Khan frown warningly, or that Yasmin had pulled her veil up and turned away.

But James saw, and said quickly, "What Jiwan Khan chooses to do is his business. We will not discuss this. I have often thought I might come and live here, make my own establishment, instead of having the old Madore Mahal opened up for me every time I visit Madore."

Atlar Khan, watching Yasmin move away, said that he thought it would be an excellent thing if Jamshyd took up residence in the Pila Ghar.

"It is shameful to let a place like this run to ruin. Take it Jamshyd, and return it back to life. I thought your father was going to do this at one time."

"Yes, he wanted to. But my mother — well, she thought it too far from Madore — and of course, like all old places, there were stories about the house — tales of lights and voices when there was no one here. The Pila Ghar was here before the year of the Great Rising in 1857 — all old houses of that time have stories told about them."

Yasmin had turned, and came back to sit on cushions in the window seat.

"What stories?" she asked. "Tell me, please."

"Tales told by servants, embroidered greatly — sounds of music and laughter heard at night in an empty house — " Jamshyd was interrupted.

"*Don't* listen to him, Yasmin." Sadik had come up to sit on a cushion at her feet.

"But I want to hear the stories — please Nawab Sahib, tell me about the stories."

"Nawab Sahib!" Sadik said before James could speak. "*Nawab Sahib.* He is not a Nawab. Not even a Nawab Zaida Sahib like me. He is James or Jamshyd. He used to be called 'the boy with two names' at school because some of the people who came to see him called him Jamshyd Khan, and all his mother's letters were addressed to James Reid. Never trust a man with two names!"

"Why not? I think it is interesting to have two names. I would like to have two names."

"You would? Then we will find another name for you," said Sadik.

Jamshyd said quietly, "I have found another name."

"What is it?"

"It is a secret, for only one person to hear."

"That means he hasn't thought of one, Yasmin. But I have. I am going to call you Yasmin Chandni — Yasmin the moon lady. What do you think?"

"I think it is a nice name," said Yasmin sedately. "But I want to choose — what is your name for me?"

She did not say his name, just turned to smile at him. Jamshyd shook his head. "It is secret."

"But I must know my name — do tell?"

"I will tell you one day."

Atlar Khan watched the three and listened and felt hopeful. Perhaps things would go well for Yasmin after all, perhaps his hope that one of these friends, whom he knew, trusted and liked, would save her from a man old enough to be her father. She was so sweet, so young to be thrown into marriage — too young. And yet her mother was married and already pregnant with him when she was fifteen, and widowed before he was born. Let Yasmin be saved from such a fate and from being sold to an old man.

He watched both his friends, but looked the longest at Jamshyd. Sadik would make a play for any pretty girl, but Jamshyd — Jamshyd was different. There had been many girls, of course there had, but he had never seen his friend look at a girl as he was looking at Yasmin. And my little sister? Too young to notice a man becoming enslaved? When did girls waken to love? She had laughed at them both, but her eyes turned to Jamshyd whenever he spoke. Well, thought Atlar Khan, let me live in hope, let this be an auspicious visit, Yasmin's first foray into the world.

There was a garden round the Pila Ghar, a garden untended for years. Presently Yasmin rose and left her cavaliers. She walked round the rooms of the old house, peering at her face in fogged mirrors, combing her hair, and found that her thoughts were turning all the time to Jamshyd. The boy with two names — Sadik was more handsome, and he made her laugh. But the other — how strange that when she first saw him she thought she knew him, that she had seen him before and could not remember where. The feeling had worn off, but still, it was he whose eyes spoke to her, who walked with her through this old house.

She found a door at the end of a passage, and opened it. It led straight into the garden. Yasmin walked out into the green shade. Overgrown and secretive, the garden received her. Bushes reached to bar her path, but parted to reveal old bricked walk ways. She wandered on and found a little marble pavilion, its carved screens half tumbled into ruin with the weight of the creepers that covered it.

Atlar Khan had caught sight of her crossing the garden and called out to warn her that there might be snakes. Jamshyd got up at once. "I do not think she heard you. I will go and tell her in case."

"In case of '*What*'?" said Sadik, also rising to his feet. "In case of just what her mother imagines I shouldn't wonder. I told you that if anything was going to happen it could just as easily happen in the long sweet hours of the day — be careful Chandni, you have a tiger stalking you, never mind the snakes."

But no one heard him, and the two figures had vanished into the tangled garden. Atlar Khan put out his hand and pulled Sadik down beside him.

"Sit, Sadik. I must speak with you. Do not say any more about second marriages. It is not, in any case, a suitable subject, and for Yasmin it is painful. I told you her father is trying to marry her off to a man older than himself — the man has a wife — Yasmin will be his second. The first wife is barren. Also, Ismail Mohammed himself is speaking of taking a second wife, he wants a son, and my mother has only given him, in fifteen years, Yasmin. So, talk of second wives will not endear you to her."

"And you are anxious that I should be endeared to her? I had the thought that it was Jamshyd you favoured."

"Yes, but my reason is a good one. He is more likely to be serious in his intentions than you will ever be. Am I not right?"

"Of course you are right. Not because I do not find your little Yasmin adorable — and I can see that later she will be enchanting. But as to being serious — you think of marriage? Oh no. I am not ready for marriage, the world is full of beautiful women, I want to pick and choose and try — until I find the one who makes me shiver. You know that shiver? When you meet the woman who makes that shiver reach both your mind and your body — Hah! That is when one marries. May such a day be a long time away from me."

"Jamshyd has felt that shiver."

"For that child? Never. Jamshyd makes *girls* shiver — he adores forbidden fruit, women of experience, the lure of the shuttered window, the whisper, the rendezvous, the only shiver he has ever felt is the shiver he feels when he thinks he hears a footstep outside the bedroom door. Little Yasmin? Sweet as she is, she is green fruit for our friend Jamshyd."

"You are wrong, Sadik. Jamshyd has been hit. I am sure of it."

At that moment, Jamshyd was pushing through the knitted creepers and bushes to where he could see a gleam of white. He found Yasmin standing near a ruined pavilion, standing so still that he was afraid she had found a snake.

"Yasmin?"

"Jamshyd — listen. What is that sound?" A choked sob? A strangled whispering sputter — it was an unpleasant sound that broke the green silence around them.

"What is it? One of your ghosts?" She sounded half afraid. Jamshyd moved closer to her, took her hand, and stood listening. He knew what it was, he had heard it before and had, some years ago, investigated the sound like choked sobbing. She turned to look up at him, and he smiled and said, "Piyari — don't be frightened by that. I know what it is. Look, come here, I will show you." He pushed at some creepers, broke some branches, and showed her where there was a marble basin, half full of leaf mould and the dried garden rubbish of years.

"See? It is a fountain — the water comes up that channel, from the river — it will be a beautiful fountain when it is cleared."

"Is this place indeed yours?"

"It will be. I will ask for it, and my father will give it to me. I have always liked this house."

"But how could you let it go to ruin, like this fountain? Why did you not take the house before?

"I had no reason to want a house before." He did not elaborate on why he should suddenly want a house, though his reason was clear in his own mind. She did not ask any more questions, only said, looking down at the water that was still forcing its way through the blocked ducts, "I would like to have seen the fountain playing."

"You will see it. I will send men up,

the fountain will throw its spray into the air, I will have water lilies planted in the pool, the pavilion will be mended and the garden cleared. It will be a beautiful place to sit and watch the river in the cool of the evening." She looked at the leaning trees, the sheltering bushes.

"Do not let them cut too much. This is a secret place."

"Secret — like the second name I have chosen for you?"

"That is not a secret — you called me Piyari — did you know?"

"Yes. But it is still a secret, known only to us — and I will be sure they do not spoil this place. I promise you."

He was promising more than just the careful pruning of a garden, and she knew it. He said, as if he did not know he was saying it aloud, "Piyari — Dil Piyari. Heart's beloved. Two secret names to add to Yasmin. Do you care for your new names?"

Before she could reply, Atlar Khan and Sadik had come laughing through the shuddery, and their moment was broken.

They were not alone again. During the

journey up river, Sadik sat beside Yasmin, with Atlar on her other side. Jamshyd sat opposite her, and watched her, taking into his mind her clear eyes that seemed to take colour from the sky or the trees, her dark, shining hair, the veil forgotten, lying about her shoulders covering the gentle curves of her breasts. He looked and did not tire of looking, learning everything he could, and while he learned the contours and expressions of Yasmin, Atlar Khan watched his face, and took hope for Yasmin. A few more meetings, and, he thought, Jamshyd would ask for her. The thunderbolt had fallen on his friend at last.

Sadik and Jamshyd did not go with Atlar Khan when he took Yasmin home.

"Better not come with us. I will not stress that I had two male guests with her — and my sister, please pull up your veil, I must appear to have looked after you properly, or I will not be allowed to take you out with me again."

In the red light of the sunset Atlar Khan escorted Yasmin back to the Jungdah House. They found their mother waiting for them in the drawing room of the

Zenana. A woman in her thirties, the Begum looked ten years younger than her age, her beauty untouched by time. Atlar Khan accepted his mother's invitation to stay and talk with her. Yasmin was sent off to bathe and change her clothes.

"Your father may arrive tonight, and will want to see you. We will be glad if you will stay and eat with us this evening, Atlar Khan?"

Yasmin, going reluctantly, said over her shoulder, "It is useless to ask him to stay, Ma-ji. He is going out with his friends to a House — the House of Pomegranates. Is that a brothel, Atlar?"

"No, you evil child, it is a place of entertainment!" Yasmin whisked out of the room before her mother could scold her. Amara Begum looked accusingly at her son.

"Who are these friends that were with you?"

"All is well, mother. They are the two oldest friends I have, and the closest. Jamshyd Khan and Sadik Khan."

She pounced on the second name.

"Sadik Khan of Chikor? The heir? Ah, if only."

She shook her head and did not finish her sentence. She had been on edge all day, she told her son.

"I must never let you persuade me again. I have been afraid all day that Ismail Mohammed would arrive early, and find that Yasmin had spent the day with you without a woman to look after her. He would be very angry. And if I had known that you were entertaining male friends, I would not have let her go. Ismail Mohammed is getting very strict with Yasmin as she grows up. He insists that she goes into purdah — veiled at all times, and in a burka when she goes out. Yasmin hates it, but he says she will cheapen herself, lose her value to any prospective husband. Truly, you men — he speaks sometimes as if she was a marketable commodity, just so much young flesh to be sold — I hate to hear him. He would have been a better father to a son — and yet he loves Yasmin."

"If he loves her I do not know how he can think of marrying her to that man Adham Khan. A man with one wife already — and a reputation that stinks."

His mother sighed. "Adham Khan is very rich — and does not ask for a dowry."

Atlar Khan laughed.

"He should be willing to pay in gold and diamonds to get a girl like my sister. It is terrible to think of. Can't you stop it mother?"

"I will try — but Ismail Mohammed is not easy."

Not easy! Atlar Khan almost laughed. Quick tempered, jealous, possessive of his wife — he wondered again why his mother had married the man. With her beauty she could have chosen any one of ten suitable princes — there was no accounting for love. He finished his drink and stood up, and his mother said, "I shall not tell Ismail Mohammed that I let you take Yasmin out."

"Surely he will not object to her coming out with me? I am her brother, and she must see something of Madore while she is here. It is not right that she sees no life at all, up in that mountain fortress of yours, Dhalli Palace. I shall speak to Ismail Mohammed myself."

His mother smiled at him.

"Ismail Mohammed has not come yet — and there is no word of his coming — he has been strange lately, his temper very uncertain. Better I think, if you say nothing. In any case, do you not start your duties tomorrow? You will have no time to spend on Yasmin. But there is one thing you can do to help me. I need a woman to be with her when she goes riding — otherwise she will not be able to ride — she is used to riding every morning in Jungdah, and it is good for her — locked up in the house all day she will grow melancholy. Find me a good, elderly woman from the hill country — these townswomen here do not, it seems, ride. I have already sent out for a woman, but no suitable person has come. I cannot let her go out until I have a woman, I fear Ismail Mohammed's anger if he hears any gossip about his daughter."

Or his wife, thought Atlar Khan. He knew that his mother was used to riding every day too, but that she did not dare ride in Madore because of Ismail Mohammed's acute jealousy. He felt a great pity for his beautiful mother. She

64

met his sympathetic look, laughed and shrugged, and then said, "Tell me of Sadik Khan of Chikor. Yasmin should not have met him, of course — but did he appear interested?"

Atlar Khan laughed at her.

"Mother! you are matchmaking! Of course Sadik Khan was interested, he is at the feet of any good-looking girl — and Yasmin is already showing signs of the beauty she will be. But the man who was very taken with her was my other friend, Jamshyd. He was quite overthrown. Mother, you are beginning to behave as other women. I did not think you would ever be a matchmaker."

"It is necessary. Yasmin is no longer a child, and there is this trouble already, with Ismail Mohammed trying to marry her off to a most unsuitable older man. I must do my duty by her, choose a suitable match, and sign contracts, to keep her safe. And what about your future? You have been a bachelor too long. Ah, my son, any girl who gets you will be fortunate. I shall look about me for one who is good enough for you."

"Mother, you do me honour — but

no. I will choose for myself."

His mother looked at him in horror.

"Wah, Atlar Khan, what are you saying — an English miss, no doubt, from the time you were in England? Do not tell me that!"

"Certainly I will not tell you anything. But do not fear that I will bring you an English daughter. Not with the unhappy example of Dil Bahadur before our eyes. The woman who is his wife has not spent above six months here in the last three years."

Amara Begum changed the subject, asking him to stay and sup with her, but he declined, reminding her that he had friends to meet. He took his leave, and rode back to his house, wondering where he could go to find a woman servant for his sister.

In Pakodi House he found Sadik and Jamshyd in the garden, arranging duty rosters. He joined them and they sat talking in the cool evening air until it was time to leave for the House of Pomegranates. Jamshyd then asked to be excused from the party that night.

"My father is alone in the Madore

Mahal until tomorrow when Jiwan Khan comes. I would like to spend this evening with him. He will think too much of the past if he is alone — this is the first time he has been back to Madore Mahal since Kassim Khan was killed. I should be there with him. Also, tomorrow we meet Jiwan Khan to be told our manifold duties. At least one of us should have a clear head and a steady hand."

Sadik laughed.

"Are you saying that your head is clear, your hand is steady? I think you should come with us, and let the beautiful dancers of the House of Pomegranates help you to get your feet back on the ground! You seem to me like a man bewitched — captured in broad daylight too."

But Jamshyd stood firm, and Atlar Khan understood, and made it easy for him to leave.

As he was mounting his horse, Jamshyd asked when Atlar Khan would see his sister again.

"God knows. My mother says that she is to be purdah nashin, she will not be allowed to ride without a woman to accompany her. I had not realised that she was old enough for these strict rules, you saw for yourself she still seems a child. I do not know how to help my mother to find a suitable woman who can ride — an older woman of course. When the Begum Roshanara comes, could you ask her if she has anyone with her who would be free to go to my sister?"

"Does the woman have to be of good family, or can she be a well-trained servant? There is a woman in the Madore Mahal, she was servant to the Begum Sara. She is Tibetan, the wife of the head chaukidar of the Madore Mahal. I am sure she can ride, for she came down with us from Dharmasala after the tragedy. She is sad, moping about the gardens with nothing to do and missing her mistress. What do you think, would she be of help to your mother?"

"Jamshyd, you have saved me. Yes, bring her to me as early as you can tomorrow and I will take her round to Jungdah House. You are a true friend. You were kind to my sister today, she enjoyed seeing the garden." He longed to ask Jamshyd what he thought of

Yasmin, but something stopped him. Jamshyd said quietly that the day had given him pleasure, and they parted.

Riding back to the Madore Mahal, Jamshyd found Sadik's words coming back to him. Was he bewitched? Perhaps he was. Even without her presence he found he could see her clearly in his mind's eye, could hear her voice and her laughter. It was pleasant to ride through the early dark, thinking of her. If this was how it felt to be bewitched, he was content. He would like to stay within the magic circles of his thoughts of her. He wished for nothing more.

★ ★ ★

Ismail Mohammed arrived in Madore some days after his family. He did not go near the house that had been rented for them, which, for the duration of their stay, would be known as the Jungdah House. He took a room in the old Serai, bathed the dust of the roads away and changed his clothes, and went out at sunset to the House of Pomegranates. There, the men who were his watchers came to him. He heard that his wife was living quietly, that the only caller was the Nawab of Pakodi. He was told that the choti Begum, Yasmin, went suitably veiled and with a woman companion, riding along the river road every day. There was no other news.

Ismail Mohammed went about the streets of Madore, talked with horse dealers, and with grain merchants, made a call of respect on Jiwan Khan. He attended various feasts, and afterwards either spent the night in the House of Pomegranates, or returned to his room in the old Serai. He did not contact his wife. Every night the watchers met with him after sunset, and gave him their news.

Like a spider in a web, he waited, and his eyes burned with impatience and hatred.

3

SHANTI, the wife of the Tibetan Chaukidar of the Madore Mahal, was glad to be sent to be a servant to the Begum of Jungdah. Worse than her grief for the death of the Begum Sara, was the boredom that had settled over her. These days she had little to do in the servants' quarters behind the Madore Mahal. She left her old husband to the tender care of his daughter, and took up residence in a room in Jungdah House. She soon became a trusted companion to both Amara Begum and the Choti Begum Yasmin.

She learned very quickly that there was only one road for the morning rides of her young mistress. The river road. Only one direction — straight down the road as far as the ford where the ferry was tied and the ferry men sat smoking their hookas in the hut on the bank, waiting for passengers. There the woman and the girl would stop after a hard gallop and rest their horses, and Yasmin would look across the wide river to where Pila Ghar showed ruined walls through the trees. Why did the girl find that old, empty house so interesting, a ruined house in a tangled garden on the far side of the river. Shanti was puzzled and intrigued by this, but it did not take her long to discover why the girl looked at the yellow house in the trees. The house belonged to the lord Dil Bahadur. Yasmin showed great interest in the Madore Mahal, and the stories of its past — and the people who lived in it.

Shanti had many stories to tell of the Madore Mahal and the people who lived there, coming and going from the valley of Lambagh. Particularly the great general, Dil Bahadur, and his son, Jamshyd Khan.

Sometimes the Begum Amara would come and sit with her embroidery, and listen to the talk. One day she asked after the wife of Dil Bahadur.

"Is his wife there now, the English woman?"

"Nay. The Begum Laura went to Belait three years since, and has not returned. Ach, he should put her away. What use is a wife on the other side of the world? He is lonesome, and the girls of the street of the harlots are not for him. He should take another wife to warm his bed and give him more sons. He is growing old, waiting for that white woman to return." Amara made no comment on this, and after a little while, folded her work and went back to her own rooms. Shanti glanced sidelong at Yasmin.

"Perhaps your mother is thinking that Dil Bahadur might ask for you as his second wife! Nay, do not laugh, this could happen, but he is too old a man for you. Let me look in the sand for you and see what I can see."

"Look in the sand? What do you mean, Shanti?"

"I can see further than tomorrow, child. My mother could look into the years ahead, and the gift has come to me. But not always — sometimes everything is blurred. The sands of time blow in the winds just as the desert sand does. But I will try for you. No, not now. After moonrise, when the house sleeps,

I will look. I look for a bridegroom, for a great prince to hang pearls in your hair and bind your wrists with silver. How your eyes gleam, child — be patient. I will tell you by the river when we go there tomorrow — there is a bridegroom waiting for you — somewhere, sometime, waiting for you." But Yasmin laughed at her.

"Oh Shanti! I am not looking for a bridegroom — I am not ready for marriage."

Shanti shook her head, disregarding Yasmin's laughter.

"Not ready? Eh, you are as ready as those apricots on that tree are ready for picking. Come then, let us pick the fruit before the wasps get it all. Ah, Choti Begum, your eyes are full of dreams — I can tell."

Yasmin wondered if Shanti could see into her mind, if she had guessed how much she thought of Jamshyd Khan, how often she saw him in dreams — day-dreams as well as the misty, confused dreams of the night. She wished that she could see him again, talk to him again, in the hidden garden. It seemed to

74

her that something had begun, something important between them, and had not been allowed to grow. Their meeting had ended too soon.

The next day, as soon as they reached the ford, Yasmin turned eagerly to Shanti.

"Did you look into the sand, did you see anything?"

"I saw a rose, a white rose — a beautiful, perfect rose. But it was not for you — the hand that held it was not yours. I can only see what is sent to me child, do not look so disappointed . . . I will try again, when the time is right."

She would say no more, and Yasmin was indeed disappointed.

The days, even with Shanti's tales to amuse and interest her, seemed very long to Yasmin. It is an event, she thought crossly, even when birds come to bathe in the fountain in the garden of Jungdah House.

She watched the birds with as much interest as if they had been messengers from — from whom? The fountain reminded her of the sad choked fountain in the garden of the Pila Ghar. Had *he* done as he had said he would, cleared the fountain, brought it back to life? Had Jamshyd kept his word? Were parrots, emerald in the sun, bathing there as they were here, and did the doves croon in the trees above the ruined pavilion as she had heard them that day? She longed to go to that neglected garden again, but no word had come from Atlar Khan, no invitation for another picnic. She knew why. If any invitation had come, her mother would have refused it. Yasmin had to go veiled now, even if she went to the stable to see her horse, or went out to sit by the fountain — the veils were light, but to her they seemed to symbolize the loss of freedom, the beginning of the imprisoning life of the Zenana.

They had been in Madore for a week, and Ismail Mohammed had not come to the house. Amara Begum grew relaxed, enjoyed the empty, peaceful days and began to hope that her husband had decided not to come to the Durbar. She accepted an invitation from the Begum of Dhar to come and watch the dancing at the banquet the ruler of Dhar was giving for the new ruler of Lambagh. She would take Yasmin, let her be seen by the mothers of sons. She would ask her friend, the Begum Roshanara of Lambagh, to provide an escort.

She had given her answer to the waiting chaprassi, when her woman came to tell her that an embroidery and lace seller had come and was asking permission to display her goods to the Begum, if the lady would care to look. The servant lowered her voice and said, smiling, "She sells embroidery and lace, Huzoor. Also she goes from house to house and meets the mothers of marriageable sons. She is a respectable woman."

"Chinibai, you are plotting. But why not? Let her come." Chinibai had been with Amara Begum since her first marriage. The old woman obviously felt that it was time to nudge her mistress into doing something for Yasmin. The woman who sold embroidery was a marriage arranger, a matchmaker. That was obvious. She would be full of flattery and gossip. It might amuse Yasmin to look at the goods and hear the gossip — while she herself could consider the names of possible young men, possible suitors for her daughter.

The woman came, a sheet was spread out on the floor of the room and she unpacked her goods. There were plenty of them, but they were of little interest. The woman's stories were more interesting. Yasmin looked at fine muslin veils, so fine that they were only a rumour over the face, and while she looked the woman talked.

There was plenty of gossip, and as it was all about people they knew, it was fascinating. But when she began to talk about the latest rows that had blown up between Jiwan Khan and his ministers, Amara stopped her.

"Roshanara Begum is my close relative. Jiwan Khan is fortunate in her — and will not marry another."

The woman made haste to put herself right.

"But of course! That is what he himself says — child or no child, he is content. His Begum has such beauty, such charm — but how not? Coming from your family, noted for beautiful girls — and look at this flower in bud here! Now, there will be no trouble finding a husband for this one — do not forget me, when you are looking about for a suitable husband. I would like to make a good match for her. There are so many possibilities for a girl of this beauty. The town is full of young men searching for wives. Even the son of Dil Bahadur! He has gone so far as to begin arranging his house. Like the male parrot, he builds his nest. He is having the Pila Ghar repaired — the garden has an army of men planting flowers! Why would a bachelor do that? Aha — he has marriage on his mind. It is said that there is a princess of a mountain state who has taken his eye — well, a good marriage after the Durbar will keep trade flowing, and help my trade too! As I said, remember me when the time comes to make a choice. I am known as a successful maker of good marriages."

Amara's face expressed only the mildest interest, but her heart had quickened, was beating even as she felt a cold tide of fear come over her. Oh no, she thought, no — it could not be what she feared. There would have been some alliance already arranged, of course there would. Had Roshanara not told her when they last met, that in the event of no child being born to her, Jiwan Khan was taking Dil Bahadur's son as his heir, after Dil Bahadur? Of course they would have arranged a marriage for a young man of such importance, he would not be left unattached. But all the same, she scented danger. She must see Roshanara soon. In the meantime she would speak with this woman, name some of the families in whom she was interested. It would do no harm if the woman carried Yasmin's name and description into respected families — and the sooner the better.

She sent Yasmin to order coffee for them all, and once she was out of the room, gave the woman a good present of money and suggested that Yasmin's name should be dropped among the mothers' of suitable sons.

Yasmin had been hanging on every word the woman said. The Pila Ghar being prepared for a bride. A princess from a mountain state? She hugged herself, dreaming, thinking of Jamshyd.

She saw his face clearly, heard his voice. He had called her 'beloved'.

There were no clouds in her sky. Life stretched ahead of her, golden, wonderful.

The next time Yasmin and Shanti rode out along the river road, Yasmin saw that the river was very low. When they reached the ford, she saw that the ferry had been pulled out of the water, and was lying high up on the banks of the river, as if it was not going to be used again. The hut where the ferry men usually sat was empty.

"Yes," said Shanti. "The river is down. Always at this time of year. For the next three months it is possible to walk over — no need for the boat."

The following day they rode out as usual, and when they came to the ford, Yasmin looked across at the Pila Ghar and said, "I would like to see the garden — will you ride over the ford with me?"

Shanti was reluctant.

"That is the Pila Ghar. It belongs to the son of Dil Bahadur — why do you want to see it? There is no one there.

The house is very old, and I have heard strange tales."

. "I have been there Shanti. I saw a fountain, and I want to see it again, just for five minutes."

Shanti looked over as if she could see through the trees. She suddenly smiled, looked slyly at Yasmin, and began to lead the way down the bank to the river.

"Follow me then, child, and we will spend your five minutes, and see the fountain."

The water was shallow, if Yasmin had walked over it would have been above her knees, no more. The banks had been cleared, and there was now a ramp made for the horses to walk up. As they went through the trees to the gate and started up the drive, Yasmin felt the silence that brooded over the place. She had not noticed it the last time, but of course there had been servants then, and the three men talking had driven the silence away. Now the silence seemed to be enclosed by the trees — the horses hooves made no sound on the soft dust of the drive. They moved through the trees like the ghosts that people said lived now in the Pila Ghar, their shadows thrown before them, blending and breaking in the broken shade of the trees.

When they came up to the house she saw that some work had been done on the doors and windows. She dismounted at the steps and Shanti got down and came to take the reins from her hands. The horses were alert, ears pricked, whickering softly. For a minute Yasmin was nervous. "What can they see? What do they hear?"

"Who knows? Horses long gone, shadows of the past. Nothing to fear. Go you to your fountain. I wait here for you. Five minutes only, or I go back over the river and leave you here in your garden."

My fountain, my garden? Yasmin felt that indeed, this place belonged to her. She walked through the trees, found the bricked path she had used before, and followed it.

The garden had been cleared and weeded carefully, but the trees and bushes still provided shade and walls of green. She stopped and looked about her. My garden, she said to herself. Here I will have roses, white roses, and here jasmine — and beneath that tree, near enough to the jasmine so that I can smell it, I will have a swing seat with white cushions so that I can lie here and be cool. She had spoken softly, and her voice seemed to her to echo another voice — a voice that told over the names of flowers and where they would be put. She looked over her shoulder but there was no one there, only the green shade and the shadows of the trees. She walked on, came to the end of the path, and saw the pavilion and the stretch of the river, and heard the soft, cool dripping of the fountain. She looked at the plume of water that was flung into the air to fall back into the water of the pool, and thought of waterlilies — and heard a sound from the pavilion, and turned.

Jamshyd was standing between the screens of the pavilion looking at her. "Are you real — or have I dreamed you?"

When she did not answer at once because she could not, he said softly, "Yes. A dream. But she looks very real."

"I am as real as you. Perhaps we are both dreaming?"

"Then let us dream on. Yasmin, your fountain is ready — and your garden is cleared — but not too much?

"It is perfect. I have chosen where to put roses — and jasmine, and a swing seat."

"Show me." He came towards her and put out his hand. "In this dream of mine, I always hold your hand. Do you dream that too?"

He saw that her eyes had, like clear water, taken the green of the trees. She put her hand in his hand without replying. The touch of her hand, the days that had passed without seeing her, the longing that had filled his mind — these things sent the dream flying down the river as he pulled her into his arms and bent to kiss her.

"Pyari — " The broken whisper joined the sound of the fountain and was lost in the falling water.

Her dreams had not moved so far ahead as his kisses — she could not recall what her dreams had held. He saw from her eyes that he had gone too

85

fast for her, and wondered desperately if he had lost her.

"Yasmin — heart of my heart — forgive me. I promise that until you tell me, I will not kiss you again. I could not help it — I have longed for you since I first saw you — sitting in an open carriage, holding your peacock feather fan. Never fear me, Yasmin, I swear that I will not behave like this again."

Her upward look was steady, considering. After a moment, he released her, and she turned away to look into the broken water of the pool. Her hand, like a flower to him, rested on the stone rim, and she leaned to see her own reflection in the water, as if she expected to see it totally changed. She said softly, "Do such kisses mean love?"

"They mean great love — truly, they mean love, Yasmin."

"You longed for me — that is the desire of the body?"

His voice was steady as he answered, "Yes. But also, the desire is for yourself — your mind and spirit. I want you for the rest of my life, Yasmin. This is too soon for you, I will put it away, and will not speak of it again. Let us return to our dream? Tell me where you want your roses, and your jasmine and the swing seat."

Yasmin turned away from the fountain.

"I think my time for dreaming is over, I was allowed five minutes. I must go."

Deeply regretting his loss of control, Jamshyd followed her back to the house. Shanti was sitting on the steps, the horses tethered a few feet away in the shade of the trees. She stood up at once when she saw them coming, and salaamed to Jamshyd with respect that was tempered with affection.

"Aiee, for youth time is like a silk cord — it stretches sweetly, and never breaks. But now the time is over for silken moments, we must go, or your mother will take my head."

Jamshyd held the stirrup for Yasmin, who swung herself up into the saddle with no effort. Looking down at him she said. "We come here every day — to the ford. Is it suitable for me to cross and sit in your garden?"

"It will be your garden when it is finished. You are welcome. In return, tell me you have forgiven me?"

"What is there to forgive? It was a different dream from mine, that is all. I was glad to see the fountain."

Had she forgiven him? He could not be sure. He said, without hope, "There is a banquet tonight, given by the ruler of Dhar — I am on duty. Do you attend?"

"Yes. They are relatives. I go with my mother — will I see you?"

"I shall be with Jiwan Khan. You will perhaps look down from a balcony — if a flower should fall near me, I shall know I am forgiven."

She did not reply. He stood on the bank and watched her cross the river with Shanti, the horses making ripples like drawn silk on the still water. Yasmin did not look back as they reached the bank. He saw her pull her veil up, and then she was gone out of sight, Shanti riding fast behind her.

He waited there, until he could no longer hear the sound of the horses, then went back to the pavilion and the fountain. But neither held anything for him now, even the memory of seeing her there, feeling her body in his arms, and her response — for she had responded, although she had been startled, he had felt, he could *swear* he had felt, an answering flame in her, a tremor of desire. His feeling of joy was momentary. Suddenly, in that green and peaceful place, the most terrible feeling of despair fell on him, he felt as if all the sorrow of the world had poured down on him. The sun had gone, the sky darkened — the silence around him was full of danger. It only lasted for a moment, then lifted, and had never been.

Was it that the place was haunted, as they said? He looked over to where she had been standing, and could not believe that anything could go wrong in a garden that she loved. Perhaps he was being given a warning. That is how he would feel if he lost her. He must make sure of her, he would speak to his father, tell him that he had found the girl he had only seen in dreams before. At last he had found the reality.

4

THAT night, dressed in their rich, full uniforms of brocade and silk, their dress swords gravely impeding any sudden movement, the three young men followed Jiwan Khan into the garden of the old Dhar Palace. It was a small palace, built before the rising of 1857, very old, but with beautifully laid out gardens.

These ceremonial evenings were almost exactly the same. They were usually for men only, but sometimes, as on this particular evening, wives and daughters would be included in the invitation. They did not join the men, they went into the private rooms of the Zenana, where sweetmeats, fruit, coffee and iced sherbets and sometimes wine, were served to them. The weather was hot, and the parties were held outside in the beautiful gardens of the palaces and houses. If there was a well-screened balcony, the women would sit there and look down on their menfolk enjoying themselves.

Unseen, the women laughed and chattered and listened to the invited singers, and compared their jewellery and their rich robes and saris.

They were not bored, they seldom had the opportunity of such evenings, the hill rulers lived in the capital cities of their states, high in the northern mountains, and in most cases, two or three days difficult journeys lay between state borders. At a Durbar there was fresh gossip to pass about, either scandalous or amusing, new brides to stare at and discuss, pregnancies to hear about, and unmarried daughters to display.

Dhar Palace was old-fashioned. The garden was laid out in the old Moghul style, with ornamental flower beds round a central courtyard, which had a raised dais at one side. The dais was for important guests and senior princes, they would be seated on low cushioned divans. Round three sides of this courtyard was a balcony, screened by pierced marble screens. It was there that the women were gathered, able to hear all that was happening, and directly facing the dais.

The chattering female voices was like the sound that comes from an aviary of beautiful, tropical birds.

Atlar Khan, Sadik and Jamshyd never entered a party without looking to see if it was a balcony or a screened veranda, or perhaps a shamiyana with a canvas screen that hid from them the beauties that they never saw — or almost never. Sometimes a screen would slip a little, or the wind would blow a screen aside — a moment's glimpse, and a slender hand pulling the screen closed was all they ever saw — but it was enough to start imagination building images.

But tonight the screens were solid, carved marble, there was no chance of seeing anyone. Jamshyd glanced up at the balconies, and Sadik laughed and said, "Jamshyd Bhaiya, do not send your heart up there — even if she is there, we can see nothing." Jamshyd thought of the morning, and wondered if he had been forgiven, and if she would send him a sign.

The Dhar Palace had been decorated for this occasion. Small clay dishes filled with oil, with a wick floating on the oil, were lit and outlined every wall, and every possible place where a small chirag could be put, including the edges of the dais.

Dil Bahadur had agreed to come to this party, as it was given by an old friend, the Nawab of Dhar. Next to Jiwan Khan, Dil Bahadur had the place of honour. Like his son, he looked up at the balcony and wondered if the Jungdah family had come. Sitting directly opposite the main balcony he felt hidden eyes watching him and wished that he had not agreed to attend. Was Amara there? His heart quickened as he looked up, then he forced his eyes away, wishing the lamps had not been placed to illuminate the dais and everyone on it. All the guests had been heavily garlanded, the scent of crushed roses and jasmin was overpowering.

Dark red, heavily scented roses lay on his pale brocade coat like blood stains. He was supposed to be celebrating Jiwan Khan's accession, Jiwan Khan his dear friend and beloved adoptive brother. Kassim Khan would have expected him to be a support and adviser to Jamshyd.

If things could have been different! If it had happened as Kassim wished, and in the way all the other rulers had come to the throne. In Lambagh the custom was that when the ruler felt that it was the right time, he would leave the throne and retire, handing over to his heir. Kassim had already decided to do this; his visit to Dharmasala was to be his last official task. It was hard for Dil Bahadur to remember how ready Kassim Khan had been to hand over to his son — and now, as well as mourning Kassim, his brain seemed cluttered with different sorrows, the absence of Laura, and the possible presence of Amara, with all the memories that the thought of her brought. Dil Bahadur, angry with himself, tugged fruitlessly at his garlands, which felt as if they were strangling him.

"Take the accursed things off," said the man on his other side. "Jiwan Khan has dispensed with his, and I am going to take mine off." Colonel Charles Windrush smiled as he spoke and dropped his garlands on the table in front of him. Charles Windrush was a friend of Dil Bahadur's from his early days in India, he had also been Jamshyd's guardian during the boy's time at school and at the Royal Military Academy in England. Charles, now retired, had come out to India and up to Madore especially for Jiwan Khan's accession. He was an admired friend of the whole Lambagh family.

The banquet was coming to an end, decanters of brandy were placed down the centre of the table, and silver dishes of sweetmeats and fruit. Men relaxed, the business of eating over, and contented belches sounded here and there from some of the gentlemen.

In spite of all the noise, the soft sound of a tabla hand drum, as insistent as a heartbeat, brought silence and turning heads. On the single note of a flute, a girl in scarlet and gold swept into the cleared space before the dais and made a deep obeisance. Several men stood up, clapping their hands and shouting a welcome. This was a famous woman. Up in the balconies a whisper went round.

"Look — it is Lara, the favourite girl of the House of Pomegranates. Our host must have filled her bodice with gold to get her to dance for him."

No one asked how the informant knew who Lara was — the gossip lines between the Zenanas and the city of Madore were long and all embracing. Yasmin, sitting quietly beside her mother, had spent most of the evening bowing and smiling at various important ladies who were known to her mother. The rest of the time she had watched Jamshyd through the fretted marble screen. Jamshyd in uniform took her breath away. She put her hand up and touched a small bruise that showed dark beside her mouth. Her horse had tossed his head back as she was leaning to adjust her stirrup she had told her mother, when the bruise had been remarked on. Now, as she looked at Jamshyd, the bruise throbbed, as if reminding her of the morning in the Pila Ghar. She shivered suddenly, and her mother asked her if she was cold. Not cold, no — burning suddenly in a fire that she could not speak about. She leaned forward to see the dance and hide her face.

Lara was beautiful. She was veiled, and yet not veiled, her face showed through the transparent gold veiling, it was like a mist across her features, a golden mist. The favourite, Lara of the House of Pomegranates. That was the House all the men visited, the women were whispering it around her. Atlar Khan had gone there on the day of the picnic — and Sadik and Jamshyd? She leaned forward to look down to where Jamshyd was standing. He was not watching the dancing, he was looking up at the balcony, she felt as if their eyes met — but that was impossible with this screen in the way. The woman next to her was her mother's cousin, Roshanara of Panchghar, the wife of Jiwan Khan. Yasmin knew her well, she had visited Jungdah, and it always seemed that the grey old fortress palace of Dhalli was made lighter and less prison-like by her presence.

"Who do you look for, piyari?" she asked and leaned forward herself to look down. "Aha, three young men. Which will you chose, little bird? Not your brother — " she paused and caught her breath, and then said quickly, "not your brother Atlar Khan — I see that handsome heart breaker Sadik there. Choose him, sweet heart, throw a white rose and let him wonder what beauty is favouring him."

"Roshanara, what are you saying — do not encourage my child in bad habits."

Amara, who had been staring across at the dais, had turned just in time to hear what Roshanara had said. The two women looked smiling into each other's eyes. Friends since they were old enough to talk, they were cousins — and called each other 'sister' in the extended family fashion of generous India. Amara moved to sit on the other side of Roshanara, who bent close to her to whisper, "You see who is on the dais?"

"I see. But only with my eyes. My heart is closed."

Roshanara moved to sit closer to Amara.

"My sister, why did you come here — even with a closed heart there is danger for you."

"It was needful for me to come. Yasmin is in her sixteenth year — how can I arrange a suitable marriage for her, with her hidden away in Dhalli Palace, among the mountains of Jungdah? Here she will be seen by the mothers of sons, and spoken about and there will be offers."

"And your heart is closed — tell me, have you looked at Yasmin with clear eyes lately?"

"What are you saying, Roshanara? Of course I look at her."

"I forget. You have never been to Lambagh. Listen my sister. In the Palace of Lambagh there is a portrait of the beautiful Muna — Dil Bahadur's mother. Yasmin is her mirror image."

Amara caught her breath. It seemed to her that she had found the answer to Ismail Mohammed's sudden hatred. Roshanara was right, there was danger for her. If Ismail Mohammed had begun to suspect . . . she said quietly, "He will kill me, my sister — his jealousy, even without reason, is terrible. I must find a good husband for Yasmin quickly, and see her safely married — then I do not care what happens. My life is over, you know that. But Yasmin — help me Roshanara, to meet mothers of suitable sons, there must be several here. I think that Anditta Begum of Chikor is already interested, she has a son, and she has been staring at Yasmin as if she could eat her. I will go and speak with her now."

She rose smiling as she spoke, as if she had nothing but pleasure on her mind, and went over to sit beside her rich relative, the Begum of Chikor, who was Sadik's mother, and Roshanara turned away from watching her to beckon Yasmin to her, asking her what she had seen of Madore, and promising to take her out one day soon to see the famous water gardens of the Tomb of the Black Queen.

"They say, Yasmin, that if you tell your heart's wish to that tomb, bending close to whisper, your wish comes true in a day — or a month — or a year." She laughed at Yasmin's interest and said, "It teaches you to be patient, I think." Her laughter turned into a sigh, and Yasmin took her hand, wondering how often this beautiful woman had been to the Black Queen's tomb to whisper her heart's longing for a child. Roshanara smiled at her, and held the kind hand closely.

"We will go and tell our wishes together, and perhaps the sleeping queen will tell our longings to one who can grant them — who knows."

In the courtyard below, Dil Bahadur and Charles Windrush had watched the dancer for five minutes for the sake of courtesy, and then turned to each other to talk. Charles said, "She is good, but when I first came out to India I saw the best. I saw your mother dance. Lara dances well, but Muna — she was a spirit moving in the hearts of men. No one who saw her ever forgot her." Dil Bahadur was astonished. To him it seemed impossible that there was anyone left alive who had known his mother Muna. With Kassim's death he had felt that a precious thread between his mother and himself had snapped. Charles saw his expression and smiled.

"I was only eighteen when I saw her. Kassim and I were of an age you know, and your mother died too young." He paused and then said, using Dil Bahadur's English name, "It is only a short twenty-one years since your mother's death Robert."

"Yes. But so much has happened in those years that it seems much longer."

Indeed, thought Charles, much has happened. He stared at me when I called him Robert.

"Tell me — are you now entirely Dil Bahudar — heart and soul? Has England lost her hold?"

Dil Bahadur answered him firmly. "Yes. Robert has gone. Faded away some years ago."

"I believe I know when," Charles said. "It was that ghastly visit you made to Jungdah and all that happened there that caused Robert the Englishman to fade and go. I am sorry, I loved the young Robert. Yes, I am sad, and yet pleased for you. No man can live two lives and be true to his essential self — and now your life is here."

"I had thought that my life was here," said Dil Bahadur slowly. "But now — since Kassim died this place seems empty to me, as if I have no place here."

Charles gave up all pretence of watching the dancer. He turned his chair so that he was facing his companion. The noise in

102

the courtyard made conversation private. He leaned close to Dil Bahadur.

"You astonish me. Your life here seems empty? What are you saying? You are Jiwan Khan's heir, an honour conferred on you by Kassim whom you profess to love so much. If he were sitting here now, what would he think of you, deserting his natural son at the very beginning of his reign when he most needs friends and trusted advisers? Jiwan Khan thinks of you as his closest friend, as well as his dearly loved brother. I had heard rumours that you were considering leaving Lambagh — leaving India in fact — but I did not believe them. Robert would never have thought of deserting Jiwan Khan and his country. Have you put away your manhood by becoming Dil Bahadur?"

Dil Bahadur's voice was a growl. "You go too far, Colonel Windrush. Watch your words!"

"I to watch my words? Not with you, dear boy, even if I have made you angry. Listen to my words and face facts. You are drifting, unable to decide what to do — it is in that drifting state that one

103

makes terrible mistakes. I see I *have* angered you, even though I speak as your true friend. Forgive me Dil Bahadur. I think of you as a dear son, I speak out of love."

Dil Bahadur covered his eyes for a moment then said, "You must forgive me. You spoke the truth, and that is never easy to accept."

"My dear friend, say no more. There can be no lasting anger between us. Let us now speak of other things. I have had very little news, there is so much going on. Tell me, is the Panchayat still nagging Jiwan Khan to take another wife? Has he made any decisions? I do not know how those old men dare to approach him on such a subject. I doubt if he will do as they ask — have you heard anything from him?"

"I have not heard anything — he has not mentioned the subject to me."

Dil Bahadur felt deeply ashamed as he spoke. What Charles had said was true. He had withdrawn himself from the Lambagh family after Kassim's death. Withdrawn himself from everything, selfishly lost in his own sorrows. His grief for Kassim was augmented by his grief for a lost wife. Sitting in the glow of the oil lamps, amongst the noisy, colourful crowd of princes, and seeing the girl whirling her scarlet draperies like red flames round her body, Dil Bahadur tried to imagine Laura sitting further down the table among the few English women, wives of governors and chief commissioners and political residents. He could not picture her there at all, because he knew that she would have refused to come with him. She would have hated this Durbar. As if a door had opened in his mind, he knew, and accepted that Laura would never come back to share his life in India. He would have to return to her, and live in England, or give her up, take his life away from her and live here, among the people he knew and understood, and in the country that he loved. Suddenly the decision was easy.

Charles, watching his face, saw the look of decision that had settled on it. After a few minutes Dil Bahadur said, "The Panchayat will have to be made afraid. I will deal with them when I get back to Lambagh. Jiwan Khan will never take another wife. His heart is filled by Roshanara, who is indeed the light of his heart. They were fortunate, I have never met two such well matched people."

Well matched, and both living in their own country, thought Charles. He said, "And you? What will you do?"

"I will live here in my own country — as long as I am granted life."

Well, Laura, thought Charles, you have lost, as I thought you would. His last visit to Laura had not been a happy one. Walking in her rose garden with her, he had asked her to return to India with him.

"You should come to this Durbar, Laura — Dil Bahadur would be so happy to see you. He is lonely, now that Kassim has gone."

She had turned on him with flashing eyes.

"Must you call him Dil Bahadur? It maddens me — his name is Robert — I married Robert, an Englishman, not some half-caste masquerading as an Indian prince. It is a ridiculous way to go on."

"Laura, my dear — you married the son of Muna."

"And of Sir Alan Reid! Why is he always called 'The son of Muna' as if it was a title — he was Alan's son too — unless *she* lied to me!" Under his sober gaze she coloured and looked away.

"That remark was not worthy of you, Laura."

"Well — I am tired of the *Indian* side of Robert always being stressed. He is not 'Dil Bahadur' by birth. It is a stupid name given to him by the Lambagh family — he is not a Prince of India."

"I am afraid that he is, Laura, by legal adoption he is an Indian prince and the heir to the throne of Lambagh."

"In fact, he is *by birth* Sir Robert Reid, fourth baronet, and my husband. It is time he was reminded of that fact. I have a letter here for him, Charles, which I would like you to give him. Also, one to my son, James. James is now twenty. It is time he returned now, and started to make his life in his own country."

She finished her words with a snap, her

cheeks were almost as red as the roses she had been cutting. He had been asked to luncheon, but he did not stay, and she made no effort to change his mind. Sadly, he thought of the Laura he had first met, standing on a hillside watching the sunrise, and speaking of Robert with love. Well, she had reason to hate India, but she had not tried to recover from her experiences. Beautiful Laura, twisting her face into ugliness by her hate for the land her husband loved.

Now, sitting beside Laura's husband, Charles put his hand up to his breast pocket and heard the letter there crackle. Laura's letter demanding her husband's return. Too late to demand. Too late for Laura. Or was it too late? She had a choice — she could come back to India — or could she? Had Dil Bahadur anyone else in his heart to take her place? Nearly three years since Laura had been here. A long time for the man that Robert had become, to live alone. But this was ground he dared not touch, he thought, looking at Dil Bahadur.

The dance had ended, the dancer was making her farewell obeisance, kneeling, her head on her folded hands on the ground in front of her, her skirts spread round her, scarlet and gold. She was pelted with coins, most of them gold, by the men, and flowers thrown from the hidden audience above.

Jiwan Khan was standing, making his farewells to his host.

The evening was over. Atlar, Sadik, and Jamshyd began to walk across the courtyard to take up their position behind Jiwan Khan, dodging the missiles that were still falling around the dancer. She ran out past the three men, smiling through her veil.

"Oho, Jamshyd! That sweet smile was for you — you have a secret tryst?"

Jamshyd did not answer Sadik. He had caught up a knot of jasmin flowers that had dropped beside his foot — accurately thrown? How could he be sure? He tucked the little bunch inside the high neck of his achkhan and every time he moved the gentle perfume of flowers spoke to him.

Very early the following morning, he rode round to Pakodi House and woke Atlar Khan. He told him that he was about to speak to his father as soon as he could find him alone, and tell him that he wanted Yasmin for his wife.

"I think that the marriage arrangers are out and about. I need someone to call on your mother, as my mother is not here. I would ask Roshanara but she is, like Jiwan, so embroiled with these feasts and festivities that she will have no time, and I am afraid of other offers going in first — will you be my messenger?"

Atlar Khan accepted with delight. He dressed and was ready to go immediately. Jamshyd rode with him and left him at the gates of Jungdah House. It was so early that the gates were still locked, and Atlar had to wait while they were opened. He thought the men on guard duty looked at him strangely, they were not the usual mounted men. He supposed that they were the night watchmen, and found them surly and slow.

When he arrived at the house his mother was still in her night robes, sitting on the back veranda of the women's quarter of the house, drinking her morning tea with her hair down and flowing over her shoulders. She looked beautiful, he thought and told her so. She thanked him for his compliment but looked anxious. What had brought him round so early? Was there news of Ismail Mohammed?

"Ismail? Is he not here yet?" Atlar Khan asked.

"No — not here — but my woman tells me that he is in Madore. I do not know what he is about, but life is peaceful here."

She laughed a little bitterly as she spoke, and Atlar Khan was glad to tell her that he had good news for her.

"I am so happy to tell you that I come as an emissary from my dear friend — he wishes to marry Yasmin!"

His mother looked astonished.

"So soon? I only spoke with his mother last night."

"Impossible. His mother is in England. That is why I have come, to make the first request, his father will call later to talk with you — if Ismail is not here, I will come as Yasmin's male relative."

His mother said quietly, "Wait — his mother is in *England*?"

"Yes. I speak for Jamshyd Khan."

For a moment, as long as it took her to turn away and put her cup down she did not answer. Then she said, "This is the son of Dil Bahadur."

"Yes. I do not think this offer will be refused! To have our families tied together in marriage seems wonderful to me, my dearest friend and my sister — keep this offer before you, mother, and turn away all others."

"The offer from this family will, of course, be considered, but I must go in — look, the gardeners are about, and here am I, unveiled and in night robes. Thank you, Atlar, my son, I will remember what you say."

She had left him before he could say anything. After a surprised few minutes he thought, well, it is a shock for a mother — the first offer for her child, I suppose — but she said she longed for a good offer for Yasmin, and surely I brought her the best. He rode off, thinking that she had been strange in her behaviour.

In Jungdah House, Amara sat down and wrote a short letter and sent it off in haste with a mounted messenger. He rode fast, through the early morning streets of Madore, until he came to the gates of Chikor House, where he delivered his letter and waited.

5

THE weather was changing. June had ended, July came in with a freakish wind and dust storms that brought sand from the desert and blew it in stinging clouds through the streets of Madore and into the green gardens, covering the lawns with a brown veil and killing the flowers. The rains were late, and people spoke gravely, as they did every year, about water shortages and famine.

Yasmin could not go riding the day after the Dhar party, and fretted, and on the second day, when the wind had dropped and she was ready to ride, her mother came into her room and told her that the Begum of Chikor had invited her to visit her and meet her daughter, Zurah. "So, no riding today — there is not time — and in any case, the dust is still blowing about and I do not want you with red eyes."

Yasmin protested when she found that

she was not expected at the Chikor House until afternoon — but her mother was adamant. She took an hour to choose what Yasmin was to wear, and the girl found it hard to be interested. She was certain that Jamshyd would be waiting for her in the Pila Ghar — but that was a reason she could not give her mother, who was disappointed in her disinterest. Amara had an air of suppressed excitement about her, but Yasmin did not notice. She endured the trying on of most of her wardrobe, with her mind entirely on the garden of the Pila Ghar, but finally the pervading air of excitement that had touched Shanti and her mother's old Ayah, Chinibai, touched her too. She submitted with good grace to the hands of the two women as they bathed her, washed her hair, and began to lay out the various oils and scents they would use on her.

Four hours later she went to her mother's rooms to be inspected before leaving. She was wearing Kemise and Salwar, the long shirt and full trousers of the northern hills. Her hair had been brushed and combed into shining order, and plaited. The thick plait hung down her back to below her waist, the end of the plait finished with a cluster of little silver bells that rang softly with her every movement. Her eyes were carefully outlined with khol, and the palms of her hands and the soles of her feet had been rubbed with sandalwood oil. The delicate smell was all about her.

Looking at her daughter, Amara thought that although she still seemed young and innocent for her age, womanhood was beginning to bloom in her. She would soon be beautiful — charmingly, innocently pleased with her own looks, seductive without knowing that she was. Yasmin smiled at her mother, and Amara could have wept for her. Instead, she kissed her daughter and reminded her to remain veiled until she was in the Chikor Zenana. "I expect you will be asked to unveil before the Begum and her daughter — perhaps the Nawab himself — as they are members of our family, the Begum is my cousin's sister, but do not unveil until you are asked to do so, and keep the veil over your head so that you can pull it across your face if, by chance, a manservant enters."

They heard the sound of a carriage, and Amara embraced her daughter again, regretting bitterly that she had to remain in the Jungdah House in case Ismail Mohammed chose that day to return to his family. Shanti pulled the burka down over Yasmin's head and let the folds of the thick cotton garment fall round her to her feet. Veiled and muffled into a shapeless bundle, Yasmin entered the carriage, followed by Shanti. The curtains were rolled down over the windows, and in stifling heat, Yasmin set off.

She waited until they had passed the guards at the gate and then, helped by Shanti she pushed back the face piece of the burka and opened a chink in the curtains so that she could see out. Shanti had brought the peacock feather fan with her, and waved it in front of Yasmin, but it only stirred hot air, and Yasmin took it from her and told her to rest her arms, the fanning was pointless in the closed-in heat. She sat quietly beside her servant, moving the fan about to watch the changing colours of the feathers and remembering that

Jamshyd had remarked on seeing the fan in her hand when he had ridden past her — before they had met. If only, at the end of this hot, and frustrating journey, it could be Jamshyd she was going to meet.

Chikor House, when they arrived outside the gate, took her breath away. Built by the third Ruler of Chikor, over two hundred years earlier, it boasted ornate gates, each gatepost surmounted by a rampant stone leopard and guarded by uniformed sowars on magnificent horses. Yasmin began to realise that Chikor must be a rich and powerful state. No wonder her mother had made so much fuss about her clothes — now she wished that her mother was with her, she began to feel extremely nervous.

The drive up to the house was bordered by flowering trees and she could see a broad paved terrace in front of the long facade of the house — it seemed a palace indeed, with many windows and arched screened doors, each guarded by men carrying curved swords which flashed up in salute as the carriage came to a halt. With Shanti's help, she pulled the burka back into place, and stepped down from the carriage. Followed by Shanti, she was led by a uniformed servant across the terrace and round to a smaller terrace, where an elderly maidservant greeted her, and took her into a room that opened off a dark inner hall. There, helped by both Shanti and the other woman, she removed her burka and Shanti smoothed her hair, and threw a fresh muslin veil over her head. Then Shanti stood back, and Yasmin, with sinking heart, followed the old maidservant down a long passage, catching glimpses of sumptuously furnished rooms on each side, and then they walked out into the glaring heat of the garden, crossed a lawn and came into blessed shade.

The Begum of Chikor was waiting for her in a pavilion built of marble, overlooking a small lake. Collecting herself, Yasmin bowed over her hands respectively, and Nadita Begum, smiling, welcomed her saying, "Come, welcome, Yasmin — here is my daughter to welcome you."

The girl who came forward, smiling and bowing over her folded hands, was about Yasmin's height, slender and pretty.

"Welcome, Yasmin Begum. My name is Zurah. Come and sit here, there is a breeze."

Nadita Begum patted the cushioned seat beside her, saying, "Take off your veil, child — there are no men here, and it is so hot."

Yasmin obeyed, and was offered a glass of cold orange juice. While she sipped it, the Begum studied her, quite openly, and presently she said, "I see you are going to have all your mother's beauty. Tell me, your father has come now?"

"Not yet, Begum Sahiba, but we expect him every day."

"Hm. Well, no doubt your mother is used to being alone, Ismail Mohammed has to travel to sell his horses." There was something derogatory in the way she spoke, and Yasmin was embarrassed. She did not know her father very well, he had had very little to do with her, and she knew that her birth had been a disappointment to him, he had wanted a son. But all the same, she felt a family loyalty to him, and wished again that she had not come without her mother. The Begum had not looked away from her once, she felt that every sip of orange juice she took, every movement she made, was carefully observed, and was sure that her displeasure of the way the Begum had spoken of her father had been noted. The Begum's next remark proved she was right.

"You are a good, loyal child — I meant nothing rude, I am of your family, child. Did your mother not tell you? Amara's mother and my mother were sisters. As girls we were close friends. But when she married again, Jungdah and Chikor seemed very far apart."

She paused, and said in quite a different tone, "Tell me Yasmin, do you have good health?"

Yasmin, confused, said that she had never had any illness.

The Begum nodded approvingly. "That is good. Your half brother, Atlar Khan also enjoys good health. Health in a family is so important, more to be valued than gold and diamonds. Your teeth — have you lost any teeth?"

"Teeth — ?" repeated Yasmin and

heard the girl behind her stifle a laugh.

The Begum said briskly, "Yes, teeth. Smile, girl."

Bemused, embarrassed, Yasmin bared her teeth.

"Good. White as peeled almonds, and even. Your eyes are clear, beautiful. How fortunate we are to have found you! I think that now I know all I need, and I am well pleased to see you and learn that you are a good, loyal and loving child, even to your father — well, well, no doubt he is a good man in his own way. He is certainly fortunate in his child. Not yet, but soon you will be as your mother, a beauty of some note, Yasmin. Now, Zurah, why do you not take Yasmin over to the other side of the lake, and let her admire our lotuses that were sent from Kashmir?"

As she spoke, the Begum followed her with alacrity, pausing to bow respectfully, glad to get away from this strange woman who looked at her with such a steady, studying gaze.

Once out of sight of the pavilion, she could not help sighing with relief. Zurah laughed, and took her hand, saying,

"Come, do not let my dear mother distress you. She is only making sure that everything she has been told of you is true. We are not going to see any lotuses, they are not in flower yet! Like you — they will be beautiful later! My mother, truly, you will love her when you learn to know her well. Now she has sent us away, so that my father can come and speak with her about the contracts and what dowry you will bring. You are fortunate, some of the mothers make the prospective brides remove all their clothes, and examine the girls from head to foot — my mother had that done to her when her marriage with my father was being arranged, his old aunts and his grandmother insisted. It is embarrassing, no? At least you were spared that."

Silent, Yasmin stared at her. Zurah saw her expression and clapped her hand over her face.

"Aiee — you do not know — you have not understood what I am speaking about?"

"Not a word have I understood."

"You must have guessed! No? The marriage maker was here, my mother has been looking for a suitable girl for Sadik, my brother, and your name was given to her, among others. When she heard your name, she immediately refused all the others — there were eight of them, and one or two were rich and important. She would see none of them, only you. She spoke with your mother at the Dhar banquet, and she liked what she saw of you, and your behaviour there. She heard that two others were trying for you, so she had to decide quickly, she could not make the customary visit to your mother before she sent for you. Well, it is all arranged now. My mother will send the messages to your mother, and the dates will be chosen — I am very excited, and so pleased!"

A marriage maker? Yasmin's head was spinning with thoughts. Of course. The embroidery woman! She was a marriage maker, nothing to do with embroidery, that was only a blind. The two offers for her — who on earth could they be? There did not seem to be any answers to her questions, so she asked one that seemed important. "Zurah, I neither knew, nor guessed, anything about this. Do you know who else is offering marriage to me?"

"Not the name, but it is said that one is young and a good match, and one is very old, already married but childless, and very, very wealthy."

Could the young man be Jamshyd? The old one — Yasmin shuddered, and said quickly, "They spoke of the old one before I left Jungdah, and my mother refused him, and swore to me that I would not be forced to marry him."

Zurah nodded. "Yes. I heard all that — it is gossip among the women, you know — and they say that your father would give you to the old one because he is rich — and has refused a dowry. As well he might, with an old wife already, and only wanting a child bearer. Faugh, how horrible. But it will be all right now. The offer we make will please your father, and he will accept it, have no fears. I am very happy to have met you, you are the sister I would have chosen."

Yasmin thought of a variety of things she wanted to say, and asked a question she felt was important. "Does your brother know about this?"

"Oh no. He will be very surprised and will make a big fuss at first, I expect. He has been refusing to marry for two years now. But when he hears about you, and sees you, it will be different. I expect my mother will arrange that he stands in the balcony above the garden when you are leaving, so that he can see you before you put your burka on."

"But Zurah, he has seen me already — seen me and spoken with me."

Zurah looked both shocked and disbelieving.

"Seen you? *Spoken* with you? How can this be — did you meet as children?"

"My brother, Atlar Khan, took me to his Pakodi House. Your brother was there, and also Jamshyd Khan."

"A picnic? Atlar Khan took you and you met and spoke with two men? Was your mother there?"

"No. I had not then worn the veil — in Jungdah we do not go veiled."

When she heard that there were no other women on the picnic and that Yasmin had gone down the river in a boat with the three men, she was both

126

shocked and envious. After a few minutes she said, "I wish I could have been there — but do not tell my mother. She is not strict, but that would be more than she could accept with approval. Oh, Yasmin — I saw your brother when I was out riding with Sadik. I ride veiled of course, and only on the back roads — but Atlar Khan went by, and Sadik called out to him, just a greeting, you know. He is very handsome, is he not? Has he chosen a bride yet, has he offered for anyone?"

"I do not think so. He says that he is not anxious to marry. It is so with me also. Zurah, I do not wish to marry. Not yet. I would like to wait perhaps a year."

Zurah shook her head. "They will never let you do that, Yasmin. We have to marry when we are this age, otherwise no one will take us, except an old man or a widower with children who wants a housekeeper. You know that old man is trying for you! Better to say yes to Sadik while you can, otherwise — Don't look so frightened, Yasmin! When my mother talks to your mother, that old man will stand no chance of getting you. Sadik is a

127

very good match you know. Did you not like my brother when you met him?"

Zurah looked as if she might take offence. Yasmin said quickly, "Of course I like him. I thought he was charming, and he is very handsome."

He is all those things, she thought to herself, but he is not Jamshyd. For a moment she saw Jamshyd clearly in front of her, and her heart seemed to turn in her breast. She blinked, and there was nothing there, only the lake and the trees, and Zurah saying, "Then why do you not wish to marry?"

"But I do," said Yasmin, speaking out of the confusion of her feelings. "Of course I wish to marry. But I want to choose for myself."

"Oh they will never let you do that, Yasmin. Never. Who knows who a girl might choose? Let me tell you, I saw, before I left Chikor this time, a trader from the silk road. They come with their camels, down from the mountains, selling silk and turquoise jewellery. This man's eyes were green and blue like the stones in the silver bracelets he was selling. Yasmin, truly, if I could have

128

chosen at that time, with him there before me, I would have chosen him — and walked behind him, leading the camels, and been glad for a smile from him — and the night ahead in his tent. But, of course, I would have disliked the life in the end. Yasmin, you are laughing at me! How unkind, when I am speaking wisdom to you."

"I was trying to see you with a string of camels," said Yasmin, wiping tears of laughter from her eyes. "A string of camels on the silk road." She put out her hand and twitched at Zurah's light silk trousers, and the embroidered silk of her Kemise. Still laughing, she said, "The silk route comes down through Jungdah. We see the men of the camel trains very often. Zurah — did you smell him? They smell just like their camels, only perhaps a little bit worse — You would not like to live with one of them, beautiful Zurah."

"Well, I know that. But *he* was beautiful — and how do you know what your choice might be? What splendid man of no means your eye might light upon? We are ready for love, Yasmin, and our mothers know that. Yasmin, I yearn to love and to be loved!"

Something true and honest in her voice and in her eyes touched an answering chord in Yasmin's heart.

"Oh yes, Zurah," she said on a long sigh, the image of Jamshyd coming into her heart again. "Yes, I am ready and longing for love. But I want to choose for myself — my heart knows what it wants." Zurah pounced, her eyes dancing, taking Yasmin's hand and dragging her to sit on the grass beside her.

"Yasmin — you are in love! I know it, you have seen someone you want — Tell me, I must know."

Yasmin shook her head, laughing again. "There is nothing to tell. Who would I see, perched up in Jungdah year after year? A camel driver, a soldier of Ismail Mohammed's forces, a horse dealer from the Rann? There is nothing and no one yet."

Zurah sighed. "Then I do not know why you want to choose — Don't you like Sadik?"

Yasmin said desperately, "It isn't like that. I do not know Sadik! I have seen this palace, I have talked with you,

I have met your mother, but I have no knowledge of Sadik. I do not even know if he has been consulted, if he wants me — I know nothing about him at all."

"But none of us know our husbands before we marry! How can we? We are not low caste girls of no breeding, we cannot walk about in the streets, looking at men — we cannot meet them and speak with them, and learn about them! We learn about them after marriage, and then we begin to know them, learn what they like, how life will be with them — after marriage, that is when we learn about husbands, and learn to love them." Yasmin thought about her mother, of the look on her mother's face when Ismail Mohammed came into her room, of the sound of her voice when she spoke with him.

"We learn about husbands when it is too late," she said, and deep in her heart she whispered the name 'Jamshyd'. Perhaps, with him, marriage might be easy. She seemed to know him well already. She had felt no strangeness with him — only a kind of sweet surprise when he kissed her.

"I want you for a sister. Chose Sadik," Zurah coaxed. But Yasmin shook her head and smiled, holding her thoughts secret.

6

SADIK KHAN, lounging on the upper veranda overlooking the garden, saw the girls leave the pavilion and begin their stroll round the lake, and decided to follow them. He knew that he would not receive a reprimand from his mother if she saw him, because she was in favour of marriage for him, and this girl, Yasmin, was a relative — young, healthy, and of good family.

Marriage did not interest him but he was curious to know what it was about this girl that had caused him to have her intruding into his mind off and on ever since he had first seen her. He had a complete picture of how she had looked, sitting in the pavilion in Atlar Khan's garden. Sitting so quietly, holding her feather fan, and barely raising her quite beautiful eyes to answer when he spoke to her.

He walked slowly, keeping well out of

sight of the girls, and when they stopped, he stopped and standing well hidden behind screening bushes, he watched and listened to them.

He could see Yasmin's face clearly in the reflecting light from the water of the lake. What colour were her eyes? They seemed to change — now blue, now green. Her mouth was so soft looking, like a rose. What was he doing, memorising a girl's face! He felt suddenly as if he had never seen a girl before. Her voice with that little shyness that made it hesitant, was charming.

He heard her words, heard her say, "Of course I wish to marry, but I want to choose." What did she mean, she wanted to choose? Who would she choose? She knew that she was being looked over as a wife for him. A storm of jealousy shook him, and, astonished, he found that he had to control himself or he would shout with rage. Who was his rival? There was no one. What had Atlar Khan said — there had been an offer made by some old man who wanted a second wife. The thought of Yasmin married to any one else was maddening him. In a storm of conflicting emotions, Sadik, happy lover, and thoughtless deserter of women, began to feel that his life had changed. There, in front of him, was someone he wanted more than he had ever wanted anyone in his whole, easy, pampered life.

The girls had fallen silent, sitting close together at the lake side, their dreaming eyes holding secrets that he could not read. Now that they were sitting, he could not see Yasmin so clearly, and at that moment he could not bear that. He had to watch her face, search it for her thoughts. He moved closer, and his careless movement rustled the bushes he was kneeling behind. Zurah started up like a partridge hearing a hunter.

"Yasmin — what was that — I heard something."

"I heard nothing — I was thinking."

Zurah was looking round, peering at the surrounding bushes, her eyes wide, scared. Sadik longed to know what Yasmin had been thinking of, so deeply that she had not been disturbed by his carelessness. But his sister would not leave it.

"Yasmin, there is someone here — I heard a crawling noise."

"Only the wind. It is growing stronger. I can feel it cool on my face — only the wind in the trees, nothing else." Yasmin stretched and lay back on her elbows, looking up at Zurah. But Zurah would not be soothed.

"No. I swear I heard someone breathing — Yasmin, I am frightened, I do not like this — someone is looking at us, I can feel eyes. Please, Yasmin, let us go — let us go quickly." Yasmin stood up at once and put her arm round Zurah.

"If there is someone here, then the kind of person who hides and watches girls is not someone to fear. They are to be pitied, poor creatures."

Sadik was interested to see that she was not at all afraid, she looked angry, and to his alarm she began to walk towards his hiding place, when Zurah pointed in that direction. He was about to be discovered in an undignified position, lying behind a bush, spying on his sister and Yasmin. He backed hurriedly, and once behind the trees began to run. The sound of his departure was clearly heard by the two girls, but they could not see through the screen of the trees and bushes that surrounded them.

"There," said Yasmin, "he has run away."

"Yasmin, you are brave but very foolish."

"Not brave really, just angry. I do not care to be spied on."

"No. It is horrible. There is a watchman — what is he doing, how did that man get in? Let us go back and tell my mother — it is not good, this. It means that I will not be allowed to be alone, not allowed to walk alone and unwatched round the lake, which I enjoy, and I won't walk freely in the garden. My mother will be very displeased." They found that the Begum was not alone. Sadik was sitting with her. The girls exchanged glances. Both immediately guessed who had been spying on them, but could say nothing. Both wondered how much he could have heard, and Yasmin found herself blushing. She pulled her veil up over her head and face, and the Begum Anditta nodded approvingly.

137

"See, Sadik, how well her mother has trained her. Yasmin, you will have seen my son from behind the screens at the parties, but he has not had the pleasure of seeing you. As we are all family members here, you may remove your veil in front of my son." Yasmin was about to say that she had already spent a day in the company of Sadik, when she felt Zurah's hand pulling at her sleeve, and held her tongue. The Begum had not heard of the picnic in the Pila Ghar and the trip down the river. Yasmin did not wish to cause trouble. She compromised by letting the veil fall from her face but kept it over her head. She saw Sadik's mouth twitch, but he hid his smile, and greeted her politely. Yasmin was beginning to wonder when she could politely leave, and was relieved when the Begum, smiling, asked her if she would like to go home, the carriage was at her disposal whenever she was ready.

Yasmin began her farewells, and left the cool, scented garden just before sunset. She was escorted through the house by both the Begum and Zurah. Her burka was pulled over her head, and the folds that fell round her were carefully arranged by Shanti. The Begum embraced her warmly and whispered, "Soon, my dear child, we will see you."

Zurah held her close and repeated her mother's words, "We will see you soon." Yasmin stepped into the carriage, Shanti followed her, and they drove down the drive, through the great gates and into the public world.

Yasmin felt that she had been living, for a few hours, in a strange land, a dream world of luxury and wealth. Perhaps it was a dream, and she would waken and find that this day had not happened, that she was lying in her own bed with Shanti standing beside her with her morning tea, ready for the morning ride. If this were so, she would only regret one thing, she thought. Her newly-made friendship with Zurah.

The gates of Jungdah House seemed very small after the magnificence of the Chikor entrance. The house was just a house, not very large, and rather dull — perhaps she had been dazzled by the surroundings of the Chikor family, where everything had seemed larger than life.

Later that night, as they sat in the cool of the garden, screened from view by a wooden trellis, she told her mother all about the visit. Or almost all. She described the richness of the palace and the beauty of the garden and the lake, and said that she had found a friend in Zurah. Her mother listened to her, asked no questions, but seemed to be waiting to hear more. Yasmin had not intended to speak about the Begum's extraordinary questions, but as the silence lengthened, her mother finally said, "What of Zurah's mother? You saw her of course, did you answer her questions?"

"Yes. Ma-ji, did you know she was going to question me?"

"Well, of course. It is the custom when a girl goes to the house of the parents of a possible bridegroom. I hope you answered well. Now tell me what she asked." Yasmin's heart had begun to beat very fast. She went through the questions quickly, and her mother listened and nodded, and said, "That was easy. You were fortunate she had already made up her mind before you went there. I am very pleased with you

Yasmin. Now tell me, my bird, what do you feel?"

"Ma-ji, please. I do not wish to marry yet — and I do not want to marry Sadik. You will not force me, Ma-ji?" Amara sighed and took her daughter's hand and held it closely.

"Piyari, we have been slow in seeking a husband for you. In three months you will have sixteen years. For you it seems that life is just beginning, but time runs on, and for a girl, time is important. I was married and widowed and carrying a child when I was fifteen. Too young, and for this reason I have not hurried you. But now — you know that an offer was made for you by an old man, and I saved you from that, and angered Ismail Mohammed. Now, as long as you are free, I am afraid for you. I want to see you married and safely disposed in a good husband's care. The Chikor offer is a very good one, the young man is suitable. What is it that you do not like in him? Of course you do not know him yet, but you have seen him, he is a very handsome man. After you are married you will begin to know him." And then it will be too late, thought Yasmin. She felt shocked and breathless, as if she had been running too fast, too far. But it was time that was running — and she was standing still, waiting for time to catch her into confusion, with her whole life being settled for her by others, settled in the wrong way. Her mother was still speaking about Sadik.

"He was in England, you know, and he is the heir to Chikor State. You must see that this is a serious offer, and for you, coming from a small state like ours, a junior state, it is a wonderful stroke of good fortune. You should be happy, Yasmin. He is everything I could ask in a husband for you."

"But Ma-ji, I do not know anything about him as a person. I feel nothing for him — Ma-ji there is someone else — was there not another offer? Atlar Khan came one day, I saw him come."

Her mother said firmly, "There has been no other suitable offer." She spoke coldly, in a tone of voice she had never used to Yasmin before. It was as if she had closed a door, and everything that Yasmin wanted was on the other side of that closed door. Yasmin could not speak round the lump in her throat. Her mother sent her to bed, saying that it had been a long and exciting day.

"You will no doubt wish to ride in the morning. Come and see me on your return, and we will speak again." Did that mean that there was still hope? Yasmin did not know, but at least she had a shred of hope to take to bed with her.

Yasmin slept badly, troubled by nightmares, and woke early. She could not stay in bed, a terrible restlessness filled her. She saw Shanti, covered from head to foot in a sheet, lying as usual, sound asleep across the door of her room. No way out there without waking her. Yasmin wrapped herself in a cotton sari and went on silent, bare feet into her bathroom, slid back the bolts of the bathroom door, and went out.

The sky was still in the deep darkness of night, but a line of light on the horizon promised dawn. The grass was cool and wet on her feet as she walked over the lawns to where the fountain whispered under the trees. She stood beside the fountain, closed her eyes, and transported herself to that other garden beside the river, the garden which belonged to her lover, and which he had gifted to her.

"Lover — lover?" the fountain whispered, and seemed to ask a question. Jamshyd? Was he her lover? She did not know about love, she told herself. She thought back to his sudden embrace and the throbbing thrill that had run through her in his arms, taking his kiss. Was that love? She did not know. All she knew was that she wanted to be with him, wanted to listen to him, talk to him, see his face, touch his hand. Was this love?

All about her now was the sound of a whisper, a voice breathing words she could not quite hear. Love — love is forever — She was enclosed in the sound, and all the whispers seemed to be asking questions.

She opened her eyes and saw the sudden dawn flooding the sky with light, and Shanti hurrying over the grass to scold her and lead her into the house before her mother found her.

7

DIL BAHADUR began to write his letter to Laura the day after the Dhar party. It took him two days. It was strange to find himself writing in English, struggling over the words, translating from the Lambaghi patois, first into Urdu, then into English. It was even harder to write the message that would, he knew, end his marriage. The end of a long dream. He read it over to himself, unable to believe that it had really come to this.

'I am not returning to England. This is my life. I told you this when I returned from Jungdah. I meant it then, and although I have been lenient with you, I am afraid that this last absence of yours — three years, Laura — has shown me that I cannot continue to live in this fashion. If you do not decide to return within the next six months, I shall divorce you. The choice is yours. You knew when you married me that this was where I would spend my life.'

The words looked back at him, black against the white paper. The end of a dream, the end of a long love. It was not ending easily. And Laura? Would she feel the pain of loss? Or would the shock of his letter wake her from her dream of life in England and send her back to him? These departures of hers, and the last three years of separation seemed to have changed his heart towards her. He felt sad and bitter. He finished his letter, signed it 'Dil Bahadur', and sealed it with the green seal of Lambagh State.

After the letter was in the hands of Charles Windrush, who was returning to England shortly, Dil Bahadur had time to think. He had no feeling that he wanted to recall the letter, change his mind. No. The thing was done, decided. It had been the right time. Now, the most urgent action was to tell his son what he had done.

How would the boy react? Dil Bahadur was suddenly full of doubts. He knew his son would be delighted that he had decided to stay on in India. God knows, the arguments Jamshyd had brought

146

forward, when, after Kassim's death, he had told him that he wanted to leave the valley, that there was no longer any place for him in Lambagh. Yes, Jamshyd had not wanted him to leave, but he wondered if Jamshyd realised that there was a possibility that his mother would not return to India after receiving the letter. Would Jamshyd wish to go back to England and live with his mother? Surely not — well, he would have to wait and see. He must speak to his son soon.

Opportunity was hard to find. Jamshyd's time was filled by his duties with Jiwan Khan, and what spare time he had seemed to be spent in the Pila Ghar. Strange, the interest the boy had suddenly developed in that old house. Jiwan Khan had laughed about it and suggested that Jamshyd was at last thinking of marriage, that he was making a house ready for a bride.

Finally, Dil Bahadur had his mare brought round and rode out along the river road, came to the ford, and crossed the river.

Whenever he took the river road, and saw the river, he remembered the stories his mother, Muna, had told him of Sara Begum and Kassim and Muna herself escaping from the Madore Mahal, hiding in the Pila Ghar — it was part of his life, this old house. He would have liked to open it up himself, and live in it — but Laura would have nothing to do with it, hated the house.

The garden, he saw, was no longer a tangled jungle. The stables were being repaired, he heard a horse stamping behind the wall, and his mare, Soni, had her ears pricked as he led her under the arch and into the stables. Jamshyd's syce was there. Dil Bahadur left Soni with him and walked down the cleared path towards the river.

Jamshyd was there. He was astonished to see his father.

"Father! Welcome. There is nothing wrong I hope?"

"No, nothing — I wanted to talk with you, and this seemed to be the only place where you would be free." Jamshyd's one thought was that this was the perfect place to tell his father about Yasmin, here in the peaceful surroundings of the place she loved. When it came to it, he did not seem to be able to find the right words, his father was restless, kept starting to speak and then breaking off to look around him. Remembering the short time he had lived in this house with Laura perhaps, Jamshyd thought.

He showed his father the fountain, the repaired pavilion with the beautiful marble screening all in place. He spoke of the work that was being done on the stables. Dil Bahadur listened and commented, and wondered when he should break in and tell Jamshyd about the letter he had written to Laura.

In the end it was Jamshyd who made it easy for him when he said, "In fact, father, the house needs very little work. Why did my mother hate the house so much? Was it the distance from Madore, or did she listen to the stories of the spirits who were said the haunt this place?"

Dil Bahadur was glad of the lead. He said: "I think it was just that there is nowhere in India that she found pleasant for long. She herself was haunted, and would do nothing to lay the ghost. She was afraid of shadows of the past, and

I could not help her, however much I loved her. Jamshyd, I have written to your mother, telling her that I do not intend to return to England." As Jamshyd started to speak, his father held up his hand.

"No, do not say anything yet. There is more. I have told her that she must come back and live with me here within the next six months. If not I will divorce her." Jamshyd's shock was great, but he said nothing, only put his arm round his father's shoulders. Dil Bahadur said quietly, "It was a hard letter to write, my son. But I cannot live like this any longer. I am neither married nor single. I must remake my life. But marriage is a hard thing to break. I have loved Laura deeply — only once was my love shaken, and I turned away from what might have meant happiness — I held fast to my vows."

There was a heavy silence after he had finished speaking. Jamshyd wondered how, in the face of what his father was obviously feeling, how could he broach the subject of his own marriage hopes? In a little while he would have to leave and go back to the Madore Mahal and dress for his evening duties — it was almost sunset now. The evening breeze had risen, the birds were streaking over the brilliant sky to the shelter of the trees for the night. His father, his eyes on the sunset colours, said half under his breath, "What a beautiful country this is — and what a beautiful evening to waste talking about a broken marriage. All this that you are doing here, Jamshyd, makes me think that you have marriage on your mind. Am I right?"

"Father, you are right. I was going to speak to you about it, but perhaps this is not the best time?"

"It is a very good time. It will help me to forget my gloomy thoughts. Tell me. Have the marriage makers been telling you stories of a beautiful bride who is longing for you alone?" He saw Jamshyd frown, and realised he had spoken foolishly. "Forgive me, my son. I did not intend to make light of what you are about to tell me. I wanted to warn you that marriage makers are in the business of marriage to make money. I would rather that you found a girl for yourself — though I do know it is difficult in this country — but if you know of a girl who you think would appeal to you, tell me, and I will make the offers — and tell you what she is like." Jamshyd laughed with pleasure.

"Thank you father. I must tell you that I have had nothing to do with any marriage brokers. Atlar Khan has done me a great favour. He introduced me to the girl. I was able to speak with her, see her . . . Father, I have dreamed of this girl all my life. It is this girl, or none other."

Atlar Khan! Jamshyd's dear friend, his boyhood companion, possibly — very possibly — his brother, had introduced him to a girl. Atlar Khan — his very name filled Dil Bahadur with apprehension. Forget the past, he told himself, it is over and cannot be altered. The present was what mattered now. The present time for Jamshyd. Atlar Khan had many English friends — all the English government officials, who had come up for the Durbar seemed to know him well. He had seen Atlar Khan talking to the wives and daughters. His fears made him speak angrily, "Atlar Khan introduced you? You have met and spoken with this girl? Jamshyd, I have great faith in your good judgement, but I must tell you that I cannot favour an English bride for you. You have seen what unhappiness that can bring — unless of course you have the idea of returning to your mother's country and living there."

The anxiety and unhappiness on his father's face touched Jamshyd. He said quickly, "No English bride, father — and put from your mind any thought of me leaving Lambagh. No, my girl is the daughter of friends of yours. She is a girl of the hills. She is Yasmin, the daughter of Ismail Mohammed and his wife, the Begum of Jungdah."

For a few moments Dil Bahadur, brave soldier, calm administrator, the loved and admired father of Jamshyd, was rendered witless. He could think of nothing to say. Jungdah seemed to be approaching closer every day. He closed his eyes for a moment, and immediately saw, clear in every detail, the face of Amara. What magic was she using to pull him back to her?

The silence became oppressive. Jamshyd was beginning to look surprised. What was wrong with his father, he had grown pale, looked like a man in shock. Dil Bahadur knew he must speak, say the correct things to this dear son of his, who was expecting his father to be delighted with his choice. Normally, he would be — there was nothing wrong with a child of those two people. Nothing wrong but his own determination to keep away from them.

Dil Bahadur found words, and expressed pleasure, and thankfully saw the happiness come back to his son's face. Jamshyd asked when his father would be able to call on Yasmin's father and mother.

"If possible, I would like you to call tomorrow morning, I know that all will be well. Atlar Khan, in the absence of my mother, called on his mother for me, and told her that I was about to speak with you, and that you would be calling to make the official offer, and the arrangements for a marriage very soon, please, my father." Jamshyd's words ran on. He would like the marriage to take place immediately after the Durbar, so that everyone in the family, and all his friends would still be in Madore. Some warning began to sound in Dil Bahadur's mind.

"Wait, Jamshyd, you run ahead too fast. There may have been other offers — suitors who have gone before you — do not build your hopes too high until we know."

"No Father. I told you. Atlar Khan told his mother that I was offering, that you would come. They will not take any other suitors now. Father, I want no marriage portion. She is enough, in herself. I cannot tell you." He stopped speaking, overcome by the strength of his feelings, and then said, very low, "Father, I knew her as soon as I saw her. My heart moved within me. There was this strange moment of recognition. I saw in her eyes that she felt it too. We have come through time and space for each other. I believe this."

Dil Bahadur found that the unease in his mind was growing. He said slowly, feeling for the right words, "Jamshyd, you are truly overcome by this passion. Take it gently, boy. Do not be in a hurry, be easy. Love — first love, can be cruel, passion dies. Sometimes it is better to marry coolly, with friendship, and let love grow in its own time." As he spoke, some trick of the light made him see the shadow of a woman dancing on the tree-shaded lawn. Only a second's sighting, and the whisper of the wind. "Love conquers all — love is forever."

He shook his head and looked at his son. He had seen nothing, heard nothing. His eyes were full of dreams. Dil Bahadur rose.

"Very well, my son. If you are sure this is the girl you want."

"Father, I have never been so sure of anything in my life before."

"Then, I wish you happiness with all my heart. I will go tomorrow morning and speak with Ismail Mohammed. I will see Roshanara Begum this evening and ask her to take your offer to Yasmin's mother." He found it impossible to say Amara's name. "We will arrange your marriage, Jamshyd, as you wish, and may joy attend you."

The breeze from the river was cold, the garden was given over to silence and shadows as they walked to the stables, mounted their horse, and rode down to the river.

8

DAY after burning day, the ceremonies, the meetings and discussions continued, as did, at night, the banquets. Tempers began to fray, the three aides of the ruler found that a great deal of their time was spent soothing ruffled feathers amongst the rulers of the smaller hill states, rearranging meetings, and organising seating so that no important figure was put in the wrong order of precedence. They counted it a triumph that no offended mountain prince had swept off with his retinue. There were some near disasters when Ismail Mohammed began to attend the parties in a constant condition of drunken anger against, it seemed, the whole world. He picked quarrels and insulted people, and was a dangerous nuisance.

Atlar Khan had spoken with him several times, had attempted to discover what was making him so unpleasant, and had been rudely rebuffed. Sadik Khan had spoken to him twice, and was astonished at his rudeness. He went to Atlar Khan and warned him. "I think the man is mad. He is dangerous, Atlar Bhai. I think you should take your mother and your sister into your house. He has insulted old Santokh Singh, the Gate Durwan, threatened to shoot him, and all because Santokh told him that he should not have a loaded pistol in his belt when he comes into Jiwan Khan's presence."

"God knows what is wrong with him — is he truly wearing a pistol? Then he must be told he cannot attend the audiences armed. I will go and deal with him." But Ismail Mohammed had vanished. Sadik had searched too, there was no sign of the man.

"He has gone, it seems. If we are fortunate, someone will kill him and save us the trouble. Atlar Khan, have you nothing to say to me? Are you not pleased?"

"Pleased? With what? What do you mean?" But before Atlar Khan and Sadik could say anything more, they were interrupted by an elderly hill ruler who had a boon to ask of Jiwan Khan.

The evening had been long, a meeting of senior ministers, followed by the usual banquet. At last people seemed to be leaving, and Atlar Khan was beginning to hope that the evening was ending when he was accosted by a junior member of his own staff. To his astonished dismay, the young man began to congratulate him on the betrothal of his sister, Yasmin, to Sadik of Chikor. Atlar Khan was tired — he felt for a moment that the sky was falling. What was this young fool talking about? He questioned him rather coldly, and stammering, the man told him that the news was common knowledge, that he had heard it in the House of Pomegranates. "A suitable place to bandy about my sister's name — never mind, forgive me, you meant well. I will have a word with Sadik Khan."

He got away from the man and went in search of Sadik, who came towards him and attempted to embrace him, saying, "Atlar Bhaiya — to think how long I have been calling you brother in affection — and now, in fact, we will be brothers, and my sons will share your blood."

"What are you talking about? Has Ismail Mohammed's madness affected everybody here? If this is one of your jokes, Sadik, you are carrying it too far."

Sadik still smiled, but he looked surprised.

"Have you spoken to your mother lately?"

"I have had no time — I have not seen her for three days Why? What has happened?"

"She has spoken with my mother, the marriage contracts have been exchanged, signed — Atlar Khan, I am fortunate, I am to be married to Yasmin. She came to our house and met my mother and my sister. Everything is settled. I thought you perhaps did not know, because you said nothing to me when we met this evening. Atlar Khan, you look quite overthrown, does this mean you do not approve?"

"Sadik, how can I approve? Two weeks ago you told me that you were not for marriage. Only two weeks. Am I to believe that you have changed your mind so quickly?"

"My mind is not the part of me that is deeply concerned in this matter. My heart has spoken very loudly. Atlar, I am deeply in love with Yasmin. I did not know love could come like this. I did not want it, I wanted freedom. Now the only freedom I will have is with Yasmin in my life, in my days and my nights, forever."

Atlar Khan had never heard Sadik speak like this. He could not believe that this was his light-hearted, womanizing friend speaking. He thanked God that Jamshyd was not on duty with them that night. He leaned close to Sadik, speaking quietly, praying they would not be interrupted.

"Sadik, Yasmin is my sister, and very dear to me. Her honour is my honour. You speak of your heart. Are you sure that it is your heart and your spirit that are engaged here, and not just the passions of the body?"

"Atlar Khan, you do your sister no honour, nor do you honour me by speaking thus. If it were lust, I could slake it easily — there are many girls. I know that you have reason for thinking of me in this way — or I would indeed be very angry. Please, forget the man I was. That man lies dead at Yasmin's feet. I, the new man, I live for her."

Atlar Khan could no longer argue with him. He had, he knew, already hurt his friend. He apologised, embraced him, congratulated him, and as they were separated by a messenger calling him to Jiwan Khan's side, he thought, I believe him. He is indeed in the grip of love. Inshalla it will last for them both. But what am I to tell Jamshyd? My mother has behaved very badly in this matter, and brought me shame. How could she accept another offer when I had already told her of Jamshyd's desire to marry Yasmin? I must go and see her, and I must tell Jamshyd before he hears it bruited about, or there will be terrible trouble. I shall go to my mother early tomorrow morning, and then I shall have to find Jamshyd.

His night was a short one. He set off for Jungdah House feeling tired and angry. Although it was very early, the heat was already oppressive as he rode up the sun-dappled drive of Jungdah House. He hoped to see his stepfather as well as his mother — surely Ismail Mohammed must be back with his wife and daughter — and sober — by this time. The more he thought of what his mother had done the more distressed he became. She had committed an unheard of error in good taste, accepting another family's offer, although he had spoken for Jamshyd earlier. In any case, he should have been told of her intention, he was Yasmin's nearest male relative if Ismail Mohammed was not at home. He should have been shown the marriage contracts before they were signed — in fact, in the absence of Ismail Mohammed he should have signed them. Perhaps the fact that he did not sign would make them null and void?

A syce ran up as he dismounted, and his horse was led away to the stables. An old woman, he knew well, came out to greet him and led him in through the public rooms to the Zenana, where he found his mother sitting on the screened veranda. She had not finished dressing, she was wearing a loose robe, and had been having her hair arranged by old Chinibai. She held hair pins, and a white rose in her fingers. She sent Chinibai away at once, but she did not look pleased to see him; she gave him a nervous glance as if he were some stranger of whom she was afraid. She did not smile, and Atlar Khan felt that there was no need to ask if marriage contracts had been signed. His mother, to his eyes, looked guilty. He asked at once if he could speak with his stepfather.

"Ismail Mohammed is not here yet, and we have had no word from him." His mother did not look at him as she spoke, she was putting the hair pins she held in her hand down on the table, very slowly and carefully, and then she studied the rose in her hand, turning it this way and that, apparently too intent on the flower to pay any attention to her son. Atlar Khan was worried as well as angry. This was most unlike his mother. He asked her if what he had heard was true.

"I do not know what you have heard, my son."

"I have heard that you received an

offer of marriage for Yasmin from the Chikor family, is this true?"

"Yes."

"And you *accepted* this offer?"

She raised the rose to her lips, then said, "Of course I accepted. It is a most suitable offer from an irreproachable family — an offer from the mother of the heir to Chikor. Your good friend Sadik Khan. Why should you imagine I would refuse such an offer?"

"Because I brought you an offer from Jamshyd Khan three days ago — before any offer from Chikor reached you."

His mother said coldly, "The offer you brought was not followed up. I was anxious not to waste time. I want to arrange my daughter's life in the way that is best for her. I am greatly pleased with the Chikor offer, and I know that Ismail Mohammed will be pleased also."

"Because Chikor is a family of wealth? You spoke to me once of Ismail Mohammed paying more attention to gaining a rich husband for Yasmin than to her happiness. What are you doing, Mother? I saw Jamshyd and Yasmin meet — there was at once a spark between them."

"I was wrong to let her come alone to your house. I am justly punished. She should not have met two young men, not members of her family — that is your fault in this. But all is well now, I have agreed with Chikor, it is done."

"And Jamshyd — and Yasmin? I tell you Mother, there is already love between them. It can happen thus. Love falls from the skies, without warning."

Amara did not look up to meet her son's eyes. The rose she held was crushed. She said sharply, "Love? What does a girl of Yasmin's age know of love? A moment's attraction of the eye — she will grow out of that. That is of no importance. Marriage is a serious affair. That is why mothers arrange marriages. Sadik's mother and I, we have, after thought, arranged this marriage. There is nothing more to be said, there is no question of a marriage between Yasmin and Jamshyd Khan, son of Dil Bahadur Khan of Lambagh. Atlar Khan, I must finish dressing now."

He thought she was going to call her

woman to show him out. He said quickly, "Mother, at least tell me why Jamshyd's offer was not considered by you? You must have a reason. This is the son of the man who rescued your family from beleaguered Jungdah! He saved my life — I know that Ismail Mohammed considered Dil Bahadur to be his greatest friend and ally. What is the reason for this arbitrary refusal?"

"Very well. This is my reason, if I have to give you one. Jamshyd Khan is the son of the English woman who does not care to live amongst us. I hear that she writes letters to her son demanding his presence in England. Should he marry Yasmin, and his mother's wishes prevail with him, he will take my daughter to that far away place — and I could not bear that. Enough now, Atlar Khan. No more argument. It is decided. She will marry into the Chikor family, and be content."

She has found a good reason, thought Atlar Khan, but there is something here that is crooked. My mother's clear eyes have never refused to meet mine before.

He sat quietly beside his silent mother,

168

and saw the faint trembling of her hands, folded together on the rose. He thought of stories he had heard whispered amongst his mother's women when they had not known that he was listening, or had thought he was too young to understand. He remembered a conversation he had heard between his mother and his grandmother, speaking across his bed when they had thought him asleep. He thought of the shadow and the hope that had overshadowed his boyhood.

Stories, gossip, dreams and hopes he had treasured when he was a boy, things he had wondered about for years, were coming together and beginning to form a truth.

His voice was very grave when he finally spoke to his mother. "Mother, you asked what a girl of Yasmin's age could know of love. Ask yourself that question. Tell me the answer. What did you learn of love with an untried heart, when you were Yasmin's age?"

He saw Amara moisten her lips, but he did not look up. He leaned towards her and gently took the crushed rose from her fingers.

"Mother — who is my father?"

Now she had nowhere to look, she closed her eyes for a second and then answered him.

"You know who your father was."

"I think I know who my father *is* Mother. Dil Bahadur is my true father, am I right?"

Now she could look at him. She had accepted what was going to be said, now there was no need to prevaricate. Her voice was very low as she answered him at last. "It is possible. I think it is almost certain."

He said, "I think that I have the right to know. Tell me." So she told him the story of the young man in the garden of her husband's palace in Bombay, and of how her mother had sent her to him, a girl of fourteen, naked, and carrying a flask of wine.

"There had been dancers, you see, naked girls — he thought I was one of them. No blame attaches to him, Atlar Khan. He was offered something freely, and took it. My mother could be blamed — but she was trying to do the best for me." She waited for a minute and then said, speaking with difficulty now, "Dil Bahadur was called Robert in those days. He had only arrived in India that morning. I had been married to Ali of Pakodi for a year, and there was no child. My mother was afraid that he would put me away, saying that I was barren. If I conceived by Robert, it would, she thought, save me. Later that night, after Robert had left, Ali came to my bed and so."

"So there is just enough reasonable doubt to make me the rightful Ruler of Pakodi State. Does Dil Bahadur know?"

"When he came to Jungdah, and we met again, he saw you, and he asked me if you were his son. I had to say no, that you were the son of Ali of Pakodi. I think he believed me — perhaps."

"He knows I am his son. I am glad. I admired him, and loved him from the moment we met. There is a tie between us, although we meet so seldom. I think he is afraid to cause trouble for me in the state — he is a great man. But now, this tangle over Yasmin. She is his child too — does Ismail Mohammed know?"

"Allah forfend. No. Listen to me,

Atlar, and learn a little about love. Love can be a dream of joy — and a chain to break your heart. I never forgot the boy in the garden. When I met the man he had become, my dreams were all fulfilled — but it was not so for him. His body answered mine, but his heart and his mind were with his wife. He left Jungdah without looking back, he knew nothing. I was two months with child when Ismail Mohammed took me in marriage, and he had not touched me, he treated me with honour. In those days he loved me. It was not only because I brought him the State of Jungdah as my marriage portion, he would have taken me without that. He loved me with all his heart, and I cheated him."

"He does not suspect?"

"I do not know. At first I was sure that he did not, but lately he has changed. He has withdrawn into himself, he sits and watches me — and worse, he stares at Yasmin — I think he does suspect, and I am afraid for Yasmin. He is a proud man. I think he would kill us both, if he discovered the truth."

She dried her eyes, and looking up at

172

her son, said, "I have done what I can to protect Yasmin. There can be no union between her and Dil Bahadur's son, and now you understand that. She will marry Sadik Khan, and will forget. I will tell her nothing."

Atlar Khan thought of his sister's lovely eyes and the way they had smiled at Jamshyd — would she be able to smile at Sadik like that? Did love strike twice? As for his friend . . . He sighed, and said half to himself, "How am I to tell Jamshyd — there is no cure in the world for the pains of love."

There was a world of sadness in Amara's voice when she said, "There is Time. It is said that Time heals everything."

"Time has not healed your heart, Mother."

There seemed to be a sound barely heard, a whisper — "Love is forever."

Had his mother spoken? No, she was silent, looking down at her clasped hands. He saw her suddenly as a woman still young, still beautiful, whose life had held little but dreams. He thought of Ismail Mohammed, and remembered what Sadik had said. The man was dangerous. His mother was right to fear him.

"Mother, I think it best if you come and stay with me. Bring Yasmin. I will send my carriage for you this evening. I have seen Ismail Mohammed, and I think he is deranged, and might harm you."

But his mother shook her head. "I cannot do that. Imagine, if Ismail comes back here and finds me gone to your palace! He would make a terrible scene, and there would be gossip of course — and that is one thing that we must not have — one whisper leads to another, and gossip grows like an evil weed. I have my own people round me here — I will tell you how secure I am. Ismail Mohammed bribed a man to watch me and report to him — what a fool he is! The man took the money, and came and told me — and then goes every day and sees Ismail Mohammed and gives him a long report of my daily doings — and will never tell him anything that would harm me. I am the last of the old ruling family, they would die before they harmed me, or mine."

Atlar Khan was sure she was probably right — Ismail Mohammed was not popular. But if he got tired of harmless reporting, and came to see for himself? He suggested this to his mother and she laughed.

"All he will find will be me with my women and the latest piece of embroidery — what else?"

He could not change her mind, and finally said his farewells and rode away with a heavy heart.

9

AFTER Atlar Khan had gone, Amara bathed her face and combed her hair into sleekness. All the time she was doing this her thoughts were scattered like frightened birds. When would Ismail Mohammed decide to come to the house? She had been told by her servants that he had taken a room and a stable for his horses in the old Serai at the north gate of the city. What was he planning? She shivered at the thought of the way he had looked at her those last days in Jungdah. She did not know how she was going to face meeting his eyes again; to look into the eyes of hatred is a terrible thing.

Behind these thoughts of fear for herself was the knowledge that one more trial awaited her. When Yasmin returned from her ride she would have to talk to her — tell her that the marriage contract with Chikor was signed and sealed and could not now be broken without bringing great shame to the family, and ensuring that she would be unlikely to make another good marriage afterwards. Jamshyd Khan and his family would not want her — Amara knew that Yasmin would not believe this, but the contract with Chikor must stand. She was going to hurt her daughter. She thought for a moment of the empty years of dreaming and hoping that she herself had spent. Was she going to give her beloved child just such a future, years of looking back at a love that had never come to lasting happiness? No, surely not. Yasmin had not tasted love yet. She would forget. Sadik Khan was a fine looking man, and according to his mother, mad with love for Yasmin. Love? Amara hoped this was so.

The morning wore on. Chinibai came in with a flat basket of fresh flowers from the gardener, more roses, and strings of jasmine blossom for her to twist in her hair. She looked at the flowers without seeing them and from habit allowed the old woman to dress her hair, coiling it up, and placing a white rose among the coils, and twisting in the chain of jasmine flower heads.

As the woman finished her task, Amara heard a carriage draw up outside. Ismail Mohammed, no doubt, arrived at last. She hoped that his temper was improved by their separation and went out to receive him, her face schooled into a smile, her eyes and mouth painted, and barely veiled by a light scarf of gauze.

The man standing by the window was too tall to be Ismail Mohammed. The tilt of that green turban — *what* was her woman whispering behind her?

"It is the Jung Sahib of Lambagh, Begum Sahiba, it is Dil Bahadur himself."

Amara caught her breath, looked at him for an instant and would have turned to escape, except that he had seen her, and was, she realised with a leap of her heart, as stricken as she was.

In silence they stood looking at each other, and years faded and were gone, forgotten.

He had started to say, "I asked for Ismail Mohammed — " but his words broke off. He was standing as if he had been turned to stone, unable to collect himself, staring at her, powerless to look away.

She was not wearing a heavy veil, or a concealing robe. She was dressed as she would be in the heart of her family, expecting to receive no man but her husband. He wondered how he had stayed away from her so long. Time and childbirth had not touched her. He could see her face through the light veil, misted and beautiful. What were they doing, standing with the width of the room between them? Only the woman servant standing behind her stopped him crossing the room and taking her in his arms.

She realised she must speak. Chinibai was standing there, staring. Amara said quickly, "I regret — my lord is not yet here. I am alone in the house with my daughter."

The suitable words, the customary words of a good wife who would not entertain a man in her husband's absence. He supposed this was necessary, and found the correct answer.

"I regret that I intruded. I did not know that Ismail Mohammed was from home." This was ridiculous, he thought. What was he supposed to say now? In his confusion he had to search for the right words. "I will return at a more suitable time." Now all he had to do was bow, and walk out of the room.

He could not do it. He ignored the servant's staring eyes, and her hand holding back the curtain for him to go out. He said, "It is a matter that should be brought to you by my — the mother of my son, but she is not here. I have come to speak for my son, Jamshyd Khan, who wishes to marry your daughter, Begum Sahiba. I trust you will forgive this break with custom. We are old acquaintances. May I discuss this matter with you?" He saw her breasts rise as she sighed.

"There is alas, no possibility of a marriage between your son and my daughter, lord. I have already received an excellent offer from the family of the Nawabzaida Sahib of Chikor. We have exchanged contracts. I am distressed to have to refuse you."

Normally he would have said something civil, Jamshyd would have been told, and someone — Roshanara probably — would have enquired about for another girl. But this affair was different. His son was so serious about this girl. In thinking of

Jamshyd's disappointment, Dil Bahadur almost forgot his own inner turmoil. She was waiting for him to go, it seemed. He would have to try to persuade her to listen to him for Jamshyd's sake — though if the contracts were signed and sealed, there was not much hope.

"Begum Sahiba — this is hard news for me to take back to my son. He is very enamoured of Yasmin. Is the contract signed? Is there no possibility?"

She said, her voice quite cool and steady, "The contract is signed. There is no question of breaking it."

As she spoke, her eyes behind the thin veil were devouring him. He was going grey — there was grey in his hair, and his moustache. But he was slim and upright as she remembered him, his voice pulled at her mind, reminding her of other words he had said, she saw his hands, and shivered with longing. She knew how his body felt, she felt his arms about her — Oh God, that after so long he should stand before me and all I can do is refuse him his wish!

He could see her eyes, those unforgotten topaz eyes — misted by her veil — or by tears? He could not tell. He tried once more to reach her, how strange, how hard she had become. He did not know if he was pleading for his son, or trying to reach the girl he had once known.

"Amara Begum. We have knowledge of the pains of love. Can we not try to avoid the great pain of lost love for our children? Let us not inflict this pain on them — they have, with their eyes made a greater contract between them than anything written on paper. Break this contract that is made, and let their love sign another — in the name of love?"

Every word he said was a blow on her heart. As she answered, her voice was almost a whisper. To him, as he listened, it sounded like the hiss of a snake.

"I have signed that contract. It is finished. Say no more, Dil Bahadur."

He bowed. "I will carry this news to my son, but I do not think he will accept it. Will you receive him if he calls to see you with Roshanara Begum in place of his mother?"

"I regret. There is nothing he can say that will alter this decision. We are leaving very soon for Jungdah to begin preparations for the marriage celebrations."

She barely knew what she was saying; any words would do if only he would leave before she broke and flung herself at his feet.

He said quietly, "I thought you unchanged when I first saw you this morning. Time has been good to you, Amara, you have held on to beauty and the suppleness of youth. But where is your heart?"

He turned then to leave her. The servant pulled the curtain aside, holding it back for him.

The curtain fell behind him, he was gone. Everything she had ever wished for in life was being taken from her again, leaving her in her private desert, eternally alone, if he was not with her. Where was her heart, he had asked. It was with him.

Chinibai came back, and Amara could not bear to see her questioning face. All she wanted now was a place where she could be quiet, and prepare for the return of Yasmin. There was no time for parrying questions, no time to weep. She went into her room, and told Chinibai she would sleep for a little time. She took out the flowers from her hair, and lay down, and because she was not as strong as she had thought, the tears that she could not control, came and would not stop.

Dil Bahadur. Heart of my heart, I love you, come back!

When Dil Bahadur returned to the Madore Mahal, he went at once to his son's rooms, determined to give him the bad news at once. No point in waiting, he felt so distressed about his failure to persuade Amara that he was afraid if he did not talk to his son at once, he would lose the courage to tell him at all.

He was sure that Jamshyd would not accept that Amara, if she chose, could not break the contract with Chikor. His offer had been the first. Dil Bahadur feared that this affair would make bad blood between Jamshyd and his friend Sadik — and between the house of Lambagh and Chikor. What a tangle. He felt helpless to assist. How changed she was — hard as a diamond and as cold. Would she have become like this had he decided to take her into his harem as his second wife? Impossible to tell. Impossible in any case. Laura would have left him at once. His thoughts stopped here, and he laughed at himself. So, Laura would have left him? She had left him anyway. Had he brought Amara into his life, he would not have spent the better part of that life alone — Amara would never have left him, and perhaps, happy in life and love, she would not have grown so hard. Amara, sweet Amara, you never refused me anything — you even accepted my departure from you with grace and dignity. Ah, Amara, I was a fool.

The knowledge that he had been the cause of unhappy years for her came to him — he thought she would be content with Ismail Mohammed's devotion. Now it seemed he could have been wrong about that.

Jamshyd was not in the Madore Mahal. His man said he had gone out early, with Atlar Khan, he had heard the Nawab say that they would go to the Pila Ghar. Did the lord Dil Bahadur want his son sent

185

for? No, Dil Bahadur decided, let him be in happiness a little longer.

Dil Bahadur could not then settle to anything. Finally he went out into the hot, breathless noon and found a slight coolness under the chenar tree, which threw a broken shade over the fountain. Half hypnotised by the sound of falling water, he played with ideas of what his life might have been like if he had brought Amara away with him, and married her. Laura would have gone, but with Amara there beside him — ?

Certainly none of the family would have blamed him — even Jiwan Khan, after the second time Laura had left him and gone back to England, had suggested that Dil Bahadur had perhaps made the wrong choice in leaving what he called 'the topaz-eyed tigress' for Laura. Jamshyd? He would have done exactly as he had — come out to India against Laura's wishes, and joined the Lambagh State forces. And the present painful tangle would never have happened. The girl, Yasmin, would have been his own beloved daughter.

The girl Yasmin would have been his

own daughter! The words seemed to be ringing in his head, repeated by the dropping waters of the fountain, whispered in the leaves above him. A great stillness fell on him. He heard Amara's low voice saying, "There is no possibility of a marriage between your son and my daughter."

Of course! He began to look back and reckon the dates of his arrival and departure from Jungdah. A baby born prematurely. A seven month's child — Rabindra's strange considering look when he told Dil Bahadur of Yasmin's birth. It was so obvious.

I am the father of Yasmin.

10

YASMIN returned from her morning ride and, seeing the carriage waiting in front of the house, thought at once that her father had come. She told Shanti she did not want to see him unless her mother sent for her. Shanti looked at the carriage, smiled and shook her head.

"That is not Ismail Mohammed. That is the carriage of the Jung Sahib of Lambagh. Dil Bahadur himself is calling on the house."

A wave of beautiful colour flooded Yasmin's face. At last Jamshyd's father had come to present his offer. Her mother would, of course, accept it. Dil Bahadur was the saviour of Jungdah, her mother had often said that — he would not be refused.

The carriage did not stay long, they heard it rumble off down the drive — and presently Chinibai came to tell Yasmin that her mother wanted to see her as soon as she had bathed and changed. "Do not be long, Choti Begum, thy mother is tired with all this visiting to and from this morning. She should rest."

Yasmin had never dressed so quickly. She could hardly sit still for Shanti to arrange her hair. She had felt tired and depressed after her bad night and her early rising. This was all forgotten now. Breathless with happy expectation, she ran down the hall to her mother's rooms.

Amara received her daughter, lying back among her silk cushions in her salon. She had re-made her face, her eyes glittered behind the rim of khol that had been painted round them, more than she usually wore, Yasmin noticed. She went forward to kiss her mother's hand and raise it to her forehead, and Amara pulled her into her arms and held her close for a moment. Then she told her to sit beside her.

"Look, my daughter, I have something belonging to you. You left it behind in the carriage yesterday, and Zurah has sent it back to you."

It was the precious peacock feather fan,

189

but Yasmin barely looked at it as she thanked her mother. Her whole being was waiting for the Begum to tell her of Jamshyd's offer. Her hands gripped the silver handle of the fan so tightly that, as her hands trembled, so the feathers moved and the brilliant colours merged and flashed. But Yasmin was not looking at the fan. Her mother was holding out a small package wrapped and tied in scarlet silk. Scarlet! The colour of marriage.

"This is for you, Yasmin. This, and much more. Please open it."

Her trembling fingers slipped, and she dropped the fan. She let it lie, while she untied the tinsel string and opened the package to reveal a small sandalwood box, its lid beautifully inlaid with ivory, showing a rampant leopard, each spot marked in ebony. She looked down at it, and looked away. She opened the box, and saw a gold chain set with small pearls and diamonds. Her mother leaned to look at it.

"How beautiful. It is a chain of jasmine flowers, your name in pearls, Yasmin."

But all Yasmin could see, as if it was

190

printed on her eyes, was the rampant leopard on the top of the little box. Fear was growing in her mind as her mother gently took the box from her.

"Even the box is beautiful, with the crest of the family — your crest now, my daughter. This is the chain that you will twist in your hair on your marriage day, Piyari. See, there are earrings and bracelets that match it." She paused, took a breath, and looking at Yasmin said, "You should look at your bridal gifts, Yasmin. They have been chosen with love."

She took the chain from the box and held it out to Yasmin. The girl looked up at her, at the chain, and said, "Chosen with love? How can that be? A chain to bind my spirit — Oh Mother, what have you done?"

Amara could not meet her daughter's eyes. Her own eyes glimmered with tears above the black lines of khol.

"I have done what I could to ensure that you are safe from a disaster you would not even understand. I have made for you a good marriage. Only a little time, and you will be happy. Believe what

I say, child of my heart's love — would I do anything to harm you? Never. I know that you believe yourself to be in love with Jamshyd Khan. Forget him Yasmin. It is an imagination, a dream of young love. Marriage is not a thing of dreams. Marriage is a strong fortress built to guard you and the children you will bear." She waited to hear what Yasmin would say, but her daughter was silent, looking away from her now. Amara sighed, and said, "This should be a time of great happiness, Yasmin. Do not turn it into a tragedy. What can I say to you that will make you understand?"

Yasmin turned to face her. "You could tell me if the father of Jamshyd Khan came to ask for me as a wife for his son."

"He came. I told him that he was too late, that marriage contracts had already been signed."

"Two or three days are allowed to change my life. Mother, will you really force me to marry a man against my will? I wanted the right to choose for myself!"

"None of us have that right, Yasmin. As to forcing you to marry a man against your will, of course I will not do that. But I will not allow you to make a marriage that is unsuitable."

"I would like to know why my choice is unsuitable. Why may I not marry with Jamshyd? I love him, Mother."

Amara shook her head. "You think you love him — that is all. Forget that thought. You must accept that there is no possibility of marriage between you and Jamshyd Khan. Apart from any other thing, I must remind you that I have exchanged contracts with the Chikor family. If I now cancel, there will be great scandal and shame — we will lose face. I will not find it easy to arrange another suitor of such suitability and such excellence. You would have to take a widower, or perhaps become the junior wife of a man already married. You would in that case, face a very difficult life."

Amara leaned forward, trying to put her arm round Yasmin, but her daughter sat so erect, and looked so distant, that she did not touch her, but sat back amongst her cushions again, her face very sad.

"Think well, Yasmin. I, your mother, beg you to accept that this marriage is best for you. Please recall how frightened you were of Ismail Mohammed in Jungdah before we left to come here. If you insist on breaking the contract, you will have to return to Jungdah, and live there — who knows how long you will have to live there before I find another suitor? Tell me, child of my heart, what is it you have against Sadik Khan? Has he offended you, has he done something in your presence that has distressed you and given you a dislike for him, something you have not told me? Tell me now, and I will at once go to Anditta Begum of Chikor and on those grounds I will break the contract. Tell me now."

The temptation to lie was great, but Yasmin had never lied against anyone. She thought of the laughing, elegant young man who had teased her, and looked so deeply into her eyes, half laughing and half serious — the man who had hidden behind trees in his garden in order to watch her with his sister. What had prevented her from finding *him* in all her dreams? What unfortunate twist of fate? If it had been Sadik Khan who moved in the hidden places of her heart and mind, how simple it would have been!

She saw now that she was not the only one who was suffering. Her mother's eyes were red with weeping, the paint that she had applied so carefully could not disguise it. She could not allow her mother to go to the Chikor family and tell lies on her behalf. Could not bring herself to slander Sadik Khan. The pain and sorrow that she felt in that moment was not only for herself.

She put her hands into her mother's hands and said, "Sadik Khan has done nothing wrong. It is only that he is not the one who has caught my heart. Oh Mother, I love Jamshyd. I know what my love is, I am not too young to know. Let me have him for my husband — I ask you for my life, Mother."

"I have never refused you anything Yasmin, but this I cannot give you. Please ask me no more. You are so young! You think Jamshyd will haunt your heart and mind for ever! Believe me, it is not so. Time is your friend. Marry Sadik, and live with him, and in a little while, you will look for Jamshyd's image in your heart, sigh a little, perhaps weep a little — look again a small while later, and you will only sigh — and soon he will be gone from you."

To Yasmin this seemed a terrible thought. If there was no image of Jamshyd, then what was left? She looked into the future with distress, and did not know how to answer her mother when she said, "Yasmin, please — if for no other reason, for my sake — will you at least think about what I have said? Go to your room, child of love, and think of what I say, and remember, I am your mother, and I would give my life for your contented happiness."

Amara's appealing eyes spoke as clearly as her words. Yasmin was already thinking deeply about what her mother had said earlier. One phrase stood out in her memory. If she broke the contract with Chikor, they would lose face — and she would perhaps have to take an older man, or become the junior wife of *a man already married*. That was the phrase that suddenly came into her mind, like a light in the darkness. Of course! This was the impediment. Jamshyd was married, perhaps a marriage had been arranged for him as soon as he returned to India from his school and army training in England. He was married — an arranged marriage, and not to his liking. Her mother would be against her daughter becoming a junior second wife, with no place of honour in her husband's household, treated like dust under the foot of the senior first wife. As if I would care, thought Yasmin, if Jamshyd loved me, if I could live with him I would not be unhappy to be his concubine.

She said nothing of her thoughts to her mother. She could not face any more argument at that time. She kissed her mother, promised to do as she had suggested — go to her room and think over what had been said.

She picked up her fan from the floor, ignoring the gold chain that lay there like a forgotten garland, and went out of the room, leaving Amara to wonder if her daughter was already beginning to be converted to marriage with Sadik. It seemed too simple, but perhaps her words had touched Yasmin's heart. Amara prayed that it was so, and fell into an exhausted sleep.

11

YASMIN went straight to her bedroom, and found Shanti seated on the floor before a carved wooden tray full of the silver sand of the river. She had been consulting her oracle.

Yasmin, looking at her, felt a stab of dismay. The expression on Shanti's face told her that whatever she had seen, it had not pleased her. "Shanti — what is it? What did the sands tell you? Was it for me?"

Shanti looked for moment as if she was going to refuse to tell Yasmin anything. Then she said reluctantly, "Piyari, they have not been very clear. The rough winds of fate have been blowing round you, and I see confusion, and distress. There is something else, and I do not understand it. There is a bird, and a beast. The bird is one I know well, a peacock with a spread tail, in all its glory. The crest of Lambagh. Nay, child, take the stars from your eyes. I know of whom you dream — but he is not the child of Lambagh — or is he? Only Allah the merciful knows. No. Over and above the bird, I see another royal beast, a leopard, wearing a garland of white blossom and I see a river of tears."

Yasmin felt a sudden flare of anger. Shanti must have heard her mother. "You have listened outside my mother's door. Your oracle is false! You make it up to please my mother. How could you play with me, I trusted you!"

Shanti brushed her hand over the sand and stood up. Dignity and hurt showed on her face, and also fear. She put her hand up to the amulet she wore round her neck on a cord and held it as she said, "Do not speak so, child. You are in the presence of power. Scold me if you must, but do not decry the voice of the sands, they are the voice of fate. I can only tell you what I see and hear. I greatly fear these voices that come to me sometimes. I do not lie, and I do not listen at doors."

She bent to pick up the tray of sand and walked to the door. "Shanti, wait, forgive me, I am in deep trouble. The river of tears you saw — they could be mine. I need your help, do not be angered with me."

Shanti put the tray down carefully, covered it with an embroidered cloth, and went back to stand beside Yasmin. "I do not think I can help you, Choti Begum. We cannot fight against what is written."

"I *will* fight. Perhaps I will not win, but I will try. Shanti, I want to bathe and change my clothes. Then, in the cool of the evening, I want to ride to the Pila Ghar. I want you to come with me."

"Does thy mother know this?"

"No. She would forbid it. Can I trust you?"

"Thy mother will certainly take my head — but yes, child of beauty, you may trust me."

The first breeze of the evening was raising puffs of dust on the road as Yasmin rode out through the door in the stable walls, with Shanti riding behind her. They took their usual route, but now Yasmin saw the shadows of the trees that bordered the road lying long across the white dust of the road, and the colours of the river had changed with the evening light, a light that was more gentle than the burning sun of the morning.

There were more people on the road at this time of day. Farmers going home from the fields, a herd of active goats being driven by a village girl, and then a string of camels which sent their horses into dancing hysteria, so that Shanti and Yasmin had to pull off the road and wait until the padding, grumbling beasts had gone by, with their tall, black-clad owners, who stared at the two women with devouring eyes. Yasmin was glad of her veil, for the first time, but she was fascinated by the people of the road, and wondered if she would ever ride this way again, have even this small amount of freedom? Her mother's plans seemed to promise a fettered life. She thought of Zurah sitting beside the lake, feeling free because she was allowed to walk alone in her own garden. How much freedom did Zurah have really? I shall have no more than she has, if I have to marry Sadik Khan.

Sadik! To her he seemed a hidden

man. Suddenly, she could not remember his face or his voice, she could recall nothing about him. Jamshyd's face and the tones of his voice were clear in her memory.

They came to the ford. The river here was now a mere trickle. They saw horses' tracks on the bank. As they crossed, Shanti said, "He is there, but someone is with him."

They rode up the drive to the steps of the house, and Yasmin dismounted and turned to look through the trees towards the fountain which she could not see. She saw that the gardeners had finished their day's work and were going towards the newly-built servants' quarters. They had planted rose trees, she could see. Next year, who would pick the flowers in this garden, who would walk among the roses in the cool of the evening if she lost the contest she was facing?

Shanti had led the horses to the stables. She came back to tell Yasmin that it was the ruler of Pakodi who was with Jamshyd. Atlar Khan, thought Yasmin. Come to admire the new fountain? Well, if she had to speak in front of him, she would do so. He was her brother, after all, he had introduced her to Jamshyd Khan, they were close friends.

"I am going to see them, Shanti. Wait for me."

She threw her veil back from her face, and walked away through the trees. She was wearing green. Her figure seemed to merge with the shadows and she vanished before Shanti's eyes, as if she was a spirit. Shanti stared, and felt for the amulet at her throat, muttering the name of Allah, the Compassionate.

Jamshyd had spent a pleasant day in the Pila Ghar, wandering in the garden, sitting beside the river, and dreaming and planning his future with Yasmin. When Atlar Khan had appeared through the trees that hid Yasmin's secret garden, he had been delighted to welcome him.

Now he stood beside the fountain, silent, staring at his friend who had just told him the news of Yasmin.

The words that Atlar Khan had dreaded to say had been spoken. There was nothing he could say now to ease the silence between them, so he waited. The soft voice of the fountain filled the stillness with reminders of happiness. Would this day ever be over and forgotten Atlar wondered.

Presently Jamshyd began to ask the questions that seethed in his brain.

"There is no question of this being a lie?"

"No. My mother told me herself."

"I do not know how to believe this. Does Yasmin know?"

"No. She will not be told."

"It is a barrier between us? I cannot marry her?"

Atlar Khan inclined his head, and as Jamshyd still waited, looking at him, he said, "You cannot marry your sister."

"I thought when I first saw her that my heart knew her. But it was something else — the same father, a recognition of the blood. I have been building my life on a dream. My father — " His voice rose a little, then he swallowed and steadied himself, "*He* told me not to build my hopes too high. Does he know?"

"No. My mother told me that he left Jungdah almost immediately after they met."

Jamshyd said bitterly, "I would have

thought better of him if he had taken her with him. Why did he not take her for a second wife? He could have done — at that time she was a widow, free to marry."

"He did not want a second wife. My mother says that his heart was entirely given to your mother. Jamshyd, do not think ill of your father. He is a man like other men, your mother had left him alone — he was carrying out a mission that put him in grave danger. My mother was in danger too — he saved her. Try to understand how it could have happened. Remember your father as he is — do not build monsters in your head."

The awful silence filled with thoughts settled on them again. After an age Jamshyd said, "I thank you Atlar Khan. You have helped me keep my father clear in my mind. Now tell me — what is to happen to Yasmin? This feeling I have for her was not one-sided, Atlar Khan. If she is not told the truth, what reason have they given her for there being no marriage between us? She must know that my father called at the house with an offer."

Atlar Khan took a few moments to gather courage for his reply. If this affair caused trouble between Sadik Khan and Jamshyd, it would be tragic. Before he could speak, Jamshyd said slowly, "There has been a rumour — but I paid no attention. A rumour about Chikor."

Atlar Khan told him it was no rumour. He saw Jamshyd's hands clench until the knuckles showed white.

"Then she is to be wedded to Sadik Khan? How did this come about? The ink is barely dry on the offer my father took to Jungdah House."

Atlar Khan felt that he was driving daggers into his friend with every word he spoke.

"Jamshyd, the affair was arranged in haste. My mother knew that her cousin's sister was looking for a bride for Sadik. She sent to suggest Yasmin, the contracts were exchanged, it was made firm. It was done to make it possible to refuse your offer without telling Yasmin the true reason for the refusal. You understand this?"

"I understand that the girl I love is to be given to that lover of many women, Sadik. Has she consented? Has she agreed?"

"She will have no say, Jamshyd. You know our customs. In this case, certainly, she will have no say."

Jamshyd said, "He will make her unhappy. I cannot bear to think about her life."

"Come, Jamshyd. Sadik is not a villain. He was looking for his future wife, as, in a different way, you were. He has changed, and he is in love with Yasmin. He will make her a good husband. Jamshyd, you must not turn Sadik into an enemy — he knows nothing of this. Believe me, he is a different man."

Jamshyd shook his head.

"Does the leopard change his spots? You know what his crest is. I know what I should do, Atlar Khan. I should go and snatch her away from everyone, and go."

"Go where, my brother? The world is a small place, where you could go, others could follow — and Allah the Compassionate knows what your life would be."

"I was thinking of another world — at

least we would be together, where no tongues could hurt us, if we were dead."

"Jamshyd, you are a man. Do not speak like a foolish child."

Jamshyd put his hands over his eyes for a moment, recovered himself and turned to his friend. "You are right, Atlar. Truly, you have always been my dear friend — and now you have more than proved this. I will find strength and sense soon. But now, I seek permission to be a coward. I must get away from Madore. I cannot be within reach of her — and however hard I try, I do not think I can meet Sadik Khan. Help me get away? Tell Jiwan Khan everything, he is my family. I will see my father before I go. I will send no messages to my dear love. Better that she should think me heartless."

Atlar Khan put his arm round Jamshyd's shoulders.

"I will see to everything. I have three month's leave coming to me, I will arrange the same for you, and I will join you. Where do you go?"

Jamshyd looked lost and confused. Where could he go? Lambagh, three weeks' journey away, was still too close — Atlar Khan saw that the young man was on the verge of breaking down.

"Jamshyd. Listen. Go to Pakodi. Take the rooms you always have when you stay with me. I will come there, and we can go up to Manamahesh, and over the Zukmi-dil Pass. Jamshyd, do not do anything foolish."

Jamshyd guessed what his friend feared. "Atlar Khan, I spoke foolishly a little while ago. Do not fear. I will wait for you, and look forward to going on a trek into the hills with you. Thank you for your great kindness and endurance, Atlar Bhai."

Together they turned away from the fountain and began to walk towards the trees. The sun had set, and although the sky over the river flamed with colour, beneath the trees it was already night, dark and mysterious, with shadows that shifted and moved as the evening breeze caught the branches of the trees and let the fading light through. Before they left the brightness of the reflecting light from the river, Jamshyd turned back for a last look at the fountain. When he joined

Atlar Khan again, his friend suddenly put out his hand to stop him. Jamshyd followed his gaze, and caught his breath. There was nowhere to run to. Jamshyd could not escape a meeting he dreaded.

The slight, green-clad figure left the shadows and drifted over the grass towards them. Atlar Khan went to meet her, took her hand and kissing it, raised it to his forehead. "Yasmin, my sister. What do you here? Who is with you?"

He heard Jamshyd say under his breath, "Oh, may God help me now."

Yasmin came forward, and he saw her face. She would say what she had come to say whether he stayed or left them. It would be better for Jamshyd if they were alone — or am I a coward, Atlar Khan thought, as he murmured that he would go and get a lantern — "Because it will be dark here in a few minutes."

Neither of the others said a word. He left them then, and Yasmin walked past Jamshyd, towards the secret garden and the fountain. After a little hesitation, Jamshyd followed her.

The last of the light was sparkling on

the fountain's arc of spray. She was standing too close to it; he saw diamond drops on her cheeks, then realised they were tears.

"Yasmin — please do not weep."

"Why should I not weep? I have reason for tears. Jamshyd, I come to ask you something that is very hard for me to ask. Please hear me out, do not refuse me."

He dug into his courage and found a steady voice for her sake. "I will hear you Yasmin. Tell me."

"Let me come and live here, in the Pila Ghar. Let me be your second wife, or if that is too difficult, let me be your concubine — please?"

He could not believe he had heard her correctly. She waited for his answer, and he took a step towards her, and with an effort of will that made him sweat, stopped and kept his hands down.

"Yasmin, I cannot do that."

"Why not?"

"Because you are too young, you do not know what you are saying!"

"I am not too young to be given in marriage to a man I do not love! If you refuse me, that is what will happen. Do you not care that I am to be given to Sadik Khan of Chikor? Oh Jamshyd, it is you I love. You love me, I know, you kissed me and told me the kiss meant love of the heart and the body. I have such love for you." There was no help anywhere for him, only his own strength. For her, he called on his will. He had bitten his lip and tasted the blood in his mouth. He found words that he knew would hurt.

"Yasmin, sweet bird — that was a dream, remember? I was wrong to have kissed you, I should not have broken into your dream. But dreams do not last — they fade with the dawn. Sweet Yasmin, I cannot marry you, but they are giving you to a good man. You will find great happiness with Sadik — and learn to dream with him."

She was looking at him amazed, pain clouding her eyes.

"My dreams do not die in the light of day — Jamshyd, what are you saying to me? You do not care for me? You do not feel as I feel? It was all only a dream?" He had done as much as he could. Now he could not speak. He looked away from

213

her, his eyes on the plume of water in the dying light, and was silent.

When he turned back, she had gone, running silent-footed through the dark trees. Beside him, lying where she had dropped it, was the peacock fan.

12

ATLAR KHAN was waiting with Shanti at the front of the Pila Ghar when he saw Yasmin coming towards them. He did not know what he was expecting — floods of tears at the very least. She had drawn her veil down so he could see nothing but the vaguest outline of her face; her voice was always husky, but it was perfectly steady when she said, "Atlar Khan, I must go at once. The night has come down so quickly, and my mother will be worried." She tried to stop him riding back with her. "I have Shanti, we will be perfectly safe."

However, he insisted, there was no question of her riding back after sunset without an escort. He was astonished at her poise. What had taken place between the two who had met in that secret place beside the old fountain? He wondered with anxiety how Jamshyd was. It seemed that perhaps Yasmin's heart had not been so seriously involved. Jamshyd, however,

215

had been shattered, he knew that. Well, it was done, seemingly they had talked together, and Yasmin appeared calmer than when she had first arrived. Once he had delivered her safely into her mother's hands he would send a message to the Madore Mahal, arranging for another officer to take over Jamshyd's duties, then he would be free to see what state his friend was in.

They arrived at Jungdah House to find a carriage and a saddled horse held by a syce, waiting in the drive. The badge of a rampant leopard was displayed on the turban of the coachman. The Chikor crest! Atlar Khan did not know what to do, but Yasmin, whether she guessed who was in the house or not, had no intention of going in. For the first time she showed distress.

"I cannot see anyone — not now." She left them, hurrying across the lawn to the little latticed shelter where she was used to sit, either watching the birds who came to drink at the fountain, or sitting with her mother in the cool of evening.

Shanti made to go after her, but Atlar Khan stopped her.

"Let her be, Shanti. She needs a little time. Go you and fetch a lamp, and then I will take it to her and see how she is."

It was only a few minutes later that he heard returning footsteps, and a voice spoke out of the darkness.

"Good evening, Atlar Khan. Where did you go with my affianced wife? — or shall I tell you where you went?"

"I rode with her along the river road."

"Her favourite ride. Has she made her farewells?" It was too dark to see his face, his voice was stern, there was a warning in it. It would be foolish to lie.

"She has said what needed to be said. It was necessary, Sadik — and now it is over."

"As you say, it is over. She will not go that way again."

Shanti came up with the lamp then, and Atlar Khan looked hard into her eyes, which met his straightly. Sadik said, "You are wrong, Atlar. This woman has said nothing. Yasmin's mother was sure that her daughter had gone that way. There is no harm. I know my friend Jamshyd, he is a man of honour . . ."

He took the lamp from Shanti's hand. "Atlar my brother. I too am a man of honour. I go now to speak with Yasmin. For her sake, to make life easier, it is necessary that we meet and speak a little tonight." There was nothing that Atlar Khan could say. Sadik had spoken calmly, and so long as he did not show anger to Yasmin, it would be good for them to speak together. Sadik waited for a few seconds, with the lamp held high, and Atlar Khan saw that he was smiling. Then he turned and walked towards the latticed shelter under the trees.

Yasmin had reached the fountain, and stood beside it as she had stood early that morning, a morning that seemed years ago. She had heard about breaking hearts — love songs and poems were written about broken hearts. Now she knew that a heart could break — she had a pain in her breast, an ache that would not leave her. She had built a dream out of nothing, and it hurt. The memory of the words that Jamshyd had said came back to her — "That was a dream, and dreams fade at dawn." The words seemed to ring in her head, over and over again, until she could not bear it, and, bowing her head on her hands, sobbed aloud, and could not stop the lonely crying.

Sadik carried the lamp into the latticed shelter, and then came to stand beside her. She had not seen him, her head was bowed so low that her heavy plait of hair had fallen forward over her shoulder and the silver bells that bound it were in the water. The first she knew of Sadik was when he put his arms round her firmly, and held her against his shoulder. He said nothing, just held her close, and presently she stopped struggling and let her head rest against his arm, her sobs grew less frequent, and at last, on a long, gasping sigh, they ceased.

"Am I the cause of these tears, Chandni? I hope not. So many tears! You have rivalled the fountain. Even your hair is wet." Still holding her closely with one arm, he was drying her face, mopping it gently with a silk handkerchief that smelled of sandalwood. She put up her hand finally and taking the silk, dried her eyes. He put his hand on her head, and smoothed back her hair, and ran his hand down her plait to the end, saying, "Your hair is as wet as a fish — these bells will not ring for pleasure if you do not dry them — let me." He undid the end of the plait, and took off the cord that held the bells, dried them carefully, and put them into his pocket.

"One day I will return these bells, you will put them on, and I will hear them ringing wherever you go, and come looking for you. But I never want to feel them wet with tears again, my bird of joy. Do you know why I am here?"

When she said nothing, he went on, "I am here to tell you how happy and proud I am that you made your choice, and chose me."

In the light shining through the latticed screens of the pavilion, he saw that there were fresh tears on her cheeks. He pulled her back into his arms.

"If you must weep, Yasmin Chandni, weep here, against my heart. Every tear you shed hurts my heart — it beats for you only — do you know that? Nay, do not shake your head my little love. It hurts me because it is so wrong that, standing here, holding you in my arms,

I am in an ecstasy of joy, while you are in the depths of sorrow. Listen to me, I make you a promise. In a month, or a week, or a day, you will have forgotten why you are weeping — and then I will make it my one aim to be sure that you never have a cause for tears again. I cannot keep all grief from you, my sweet bird, but I will be sure that I cause you none."

She repeated his words, "In a month — or a week — or a day — I know those words. They are the promise from the tomb of the Black Queen — Have you been there?" She had lifted her head, and frowning a little, looked up into his face.

"I know the garden, and the tomb well — but it is a place where women go to ask for favours. You do not have to do that. I have given you my promise. Remember what I have said."

In a month — or a week — or a day. I will forget. That is Sadik's promise. Perhaps I will forget, all this hot pain, this desperate longing. She could not know if there was going to be forgetfulness or not. She only knew that she found comfort in the strong arms that held her, in the firm words he spoke. She let her head drop against his shoulder and was still.

In the house, in the privacy of the Zenana reception room, Anditta Begum of Chikor and Amara had concluded their business over suitable dates, and the locale of the marriage festivities. Anditta had agreed wholeheartedly that these should take place in Pakodi.

"You will not be returning to Jungdah, my sister?" Amara's eyes veiled themselves for a moment.

"No. I will go to Panchghar after the marriage — and stay there with my sister and her husband the ruler. I regret to say this to you, but . . . " She hesitated, wondering suddenly how well she knew Anditta.

Would what she had to say do any damage to Yasmin's prospects, stop the marriage even? She need not have worried. Anditta Begum finished her sentence for her.

"Your marriage is over. Yes, I understand that. There will be no fingers poked in scorn at you, my sister. You have borne much. But he will never divorce you Amara — you know that."

Amara shrugged, and met her cousin's understanding eyes.

"So he will not divorce me. I can live and breathe a clearer air if I am out of his presence. I will be at peace."

The topaz eyes glinted as she spoke, flashed a little, and then she looked away. There is no peace in your heart Amara, thought the other woman, and felt pity for her. The stories about Ismail Mohammed were legion, and Anditta Begum had heard them all. She stood up and embraced Amara.

"You will live in Panchghar. That is sensible and good, my sister. Panchghar is only a short, easy journey from Chikor. We will meet often, and re-live old days. I wish for you the happiness you seek." Her eyes were questioning, she waited hopefully, but Amara's eyes gave her no answers. Anditta smiled and said, "Ah well, my dear sister. We have completed a good thing for our children this evening. I will see you in Pakodi in one month's time.

We will both be very busy between now and then."

Sadik, standing beside the fountain with Yasmin in his arms, looked up when a voice called his name quietly from the shadows.

"Your mother wishes to leave now — let me take Yasmin to Amara Begum."

Atlar Khan stepped forward as he spoke, but Sadik said, "I ask for one moment longer." Atlar waited. Sadik looked down at Yasmin.

"You have found some comfort, I think? That is good. Look up my bird — the moon is there. I shall see you again when this moon has gone and there is a new moon in the skies. Remember me, and do not drive me out of your heart with other memories. I love you, Yasmin, I give you my heart. You will give me yours when the new moon rises." He walked away from her then, and left her looking after his tall, striding figure. Was that her future, that tall man? She only knew that in the midst of sorrow, she still missed the comfort of his arms.

Atlar Khan came to her. "Your mother

is waiting for you, Yasmin — come with me."

Yasmin stood before her mother. Her hair was wet and dishevelled, her face was stained with tears and her eyes were swollen, but she stood straight and met her mother's gaze unflinchingly. Amara asked no questions. She put her arms round her daughter and kissed her, and went with her to her bedroom, where Shanti was stirring some powder into a glass of warm milk. Yasmin drank half of it, and then with the glass still in her hand, began to fall asleep. Amara took the glass away, Shanti let down the mosquito curtains, and Amara went back to her own room, leaving Shanti to bolt the bathroom door, and turn the key as well. She took the key and put it in her bosom, and then lay down across the bedroom door to sleep.

Amara went to bed, and the lamp in her room burned all night while she lay thinking of the past, and planning the future — and preparing in her mind for the journey to Pakodi and the marriage that would leave her without her child.

225

13

THROUGH the heat of that afternoon, Dil Bahadur rode back to Jungdah House. The house was wrapped in a siesta silence; he feared that no one would hear his call, but a syce came out from the stables immediately, and said he would go and rouse a servant. Dil Bahadur took the precaution of asking once more for the Nawab Ismail Mohammed, to ask for the Begum directly would be unwise. He stood on the veranda waiting, wondering if he would be turned away, if once more the reply would be that the man of the house was not there — but presently he heard slippered feet approaching, and the same old woman who had opened the door to him in the morning came and held back the screen over the door so that he could enter.

Amara was sitting on a cushioned divan, her feet tucked under her. She was veiled, but, as before, it was a light veiling. He saw the contour of her eyes and lips through the muslin, but could not see her expression. She gestured to a seat on the opposite side of the room, and said quietly, "You are welcome, Dil Bahadur. I regret, but my husband is not here. I hope that you have not come to speak about the marriage of Yasmin. My answer must be the same as it was this morning — however hard and cold that seems."

The servant had left the room but he was sure that she must be on the other side of the curtained door. He glanced at the curtain as he said, "I know now more than I knew this morning. I understand why this marriage cannot be."

He saw her slender, long-fingered hands clench themselves together. She was taut as a stretched wire and he would have given anything to move across the room and take her hands in his. He said, "I was wrong in what I said when I left you this morning — but I did not know then. I hope you understand?"

He thought that she smiled behind her veil. She said, "You asked me where my heart was. It is where it always was, Lord."

To hold a conversation, sitting so far from her, with ears and eyes all round them, was terrible. But he was determined to speak, these were presumably trusted servants. "You know that I would have stayed in Jungdah if I had known what had happened — why did you keep this thing from me?"

She sighed, and again he was sure that she was smiling at him. "Would you have listened to me, Lord? At that time your mind and heart were very occupied — but even so, Dil Bahadur, at the time of your departure I did not know anything — if you had perhaps waited another week — I would have told you, I think. Tell me, Lord, where is your wife?"

"She is in England. It is now almost three years since I have seen her." He waited, but she said, nothing, only he heard her sigh again, and he said, "I do not think she will return. I have given her six months." He saw her veiled face bow over her hands, but she was still silent. He asked, "Where will you be in six month's time, Amara Begum?"

"I will be, if God pleases, in Panchghar with my sister." Was she breaking with Ismail Mohammed? She seemed to read his mind, and said, "Ismail Mohammed will be in Jungdah. I cannot continue living there with him. I must tell you this. He has changed. He wishes to own my soul, and I have nothing to give him."

He saw that her hands were tightly clenched again. Hands of such slender grace that he had kissed through a long ago night, when kisses were given and taken with such pleasure — and now he must sit like an image, and she, veiled, and it seemed as far from him as if they had never met as lovers. Even her voice was strained as she said, "He is cruelly changed, and it is my fault. He asks what would be so easy for me to give — so easy to give with pleasure, but not to him. It is unjust, but I cannot help it. My spirit and my heart are gone elsewhere."

She glanced then at the curtain, as if she had heard something. He saw fear in the movement, and she said, "Dil Bahadur, your horse is outside. It is

229

better now for me if you leave me."

He stood up at once, hating the circumstances in which he was placed. To run, like a seducer, warned of the coming of the husband — it was shaming. He could not say farewell to her, better to turn and go, but at the door he stopped and looking back, said quietly, "Perhaps — in Panchghar? In six months?"

Her reply was muffled, she was looking at the curtain again, and the words he thought he heard gave him no pleasure. Had he heard aright? Had she really given him such an uncertain answer? The words he thought he heard were, "Perhaps — who can say?"

Then he was through the door and out into the brilliant, blazing afternoon sun, riding away from everything he wanted.

Five minutes after his departure, Chinibai came to tell Amara that one of the men on duty at the gate wished to speak with her. He was brought in, one of her own men, a man she trusted.

"What is it Parta Sing?"

He was a man of Jungdah. She spoke to him in his own tongue. He smiled briefly as he salaamed her. Then he told her that lately, a watcher had been waiting in the shadows outside her gate. "A man on a horse. One night at the front gate, then, maybe, two or three nights outside the stable gate. He never tries to enter, he does not dismount, he does nothing. But he is always, for the last week, at one gate or the other. Sometimes he stays until very late — but he always come at the same time, he comes soon after sunset. He comes as soon as it is full dark."

"But who — is it one of Ismail Mohammed's men?"

"Nay, Huzoor. Not one of his men." The man paused, looking uncomfortable. It suddenly came to her that he was afraid, and she began to be aware of a cold, creeping fear running through her.

"Well then, who is it?"

"Lady, it is himself — the Nawab Sahib Ismail Mohammed — and we are afraid for you. He is not well, Sahiba. He sits there among the trees, like a man of stone on a stone horse. He seemed like part of the shadows when we first saw him, and when he rides away it is as if a darkness has lifted. We, your servants, are very afraid for you. We do not think you should remain here alone, with the Choti Begum. You should go to the mahal of your son Atlar Khan."

To Atlar's Palace, where Jamshyd would certainly be able to come easily. Impossible, all her plans would be ruined. She said firmly, "Very well, prepare to leave tomorrow morning, early. Do as much of the preparations for going as you can at once. Then when it is dark, mount the guard as usual. When the Nawab rides away, finish your preparations. We go to Panchghar. We will leave as soon after dawn as we can be ready."

The man saluted and hurried out. Amara did not have to give any orders to her women servants. Chinibai would do that. She would be telling Shanti to start packing at once. It only remained for her to call Yasmin and tell her that they were leaving — she imagined how unwelcome the change of plan would be to her daughter, she was probably hoping, with the endless hope of youth, that everything would come right if she stayed in Madore. Poor child. But the fear that filled Amara's mind did not allow her to think too much of how Yasmin would feel about the unexpected journey. The thought of Ismail Mohammed hiding in the shadows outside the gate was terrifying. She had not been able to blot out the memory of the look she had seen in his eyes just before they had left to come to Madore. She hurried down to her daughter's room, calling to her as she went.

It was then that she discovered that both Shanti and Yasmin were not in the house.

Their horses were gone too. Riding at this time, before the air had cooled — what had possessed the girl? And where had she gone? Terrible thoughts of an elopement, or a kidnapping, began to fill her mind. She was trying to bring some order into her thoughts, and decide what she had better do, when a carriage rumbled up the drive, and she saw the uniforms and the outriders — one of whom she recognised. The Begum of Chikor had come to call on her, and had brought her son Sadik Khan with her. Smiling with stiff lips, Amara welcomed her guests, apologised for her daughter, who had gone out for a late ride but would be back very soon. Cold drinks, small dishes of dried fruit and salted nuts were brought, and the civilities of a conversation started, while Amara struggled to disguise her fears. The Begum asked about her plans when the Durbar ended, and Sadik sat quietly, watching the women. An hour passed, they had finished their drinks, and the swift darkness of the night had fallen on the garden, when Amara heard the sound of horses coming up to the house. Thank God — it must be Yasmin — but where had she been, what state was she going to be in? Some dreadful thing must have happened to keep her out so long. Amara stood up, but Sadik Khan was before her.

"Sit, Begum Sahiba, stay with my mother. I will go and bring Yasmin in."

There was nothing Amara could do. She sank down again among her cushions, and saw Anditta Begum's kind eyes examining her.

"What is it, Amara? You have been so nervous all this hour — I can guess why."

Amara hoped that one of her fears could not be guessed at. She was convinced that Yasmin must have gone to Jamshyd Khan. But it seemed that Anditta Begum had not thought of anything like that.

"It was thoughtless of the child to stay out so late when she knew you must be worried. You were afraid that Ismail Mohammed might have taken her? Truly, life is very difficult for us women, shut away in our homes with nothing to do but worry about our children — and indeed our husbands. You have had a long road of troubles, my dear Amara, my heart has been sore for you. But see how well everything has turned out now. Yasmin will be happy, I promise you, in our household. She will not be treated as a daughter-in-law, she is already in my heart as a daughter, and Zurah loves her as a sister. All is well now, Amara."

Amara sat smiling beside this kind woman, straining her ears to hear what was happening in the garden. Where had Yasmin been? When were these people going to leave her and let her find answers to all her questions.

When Dil Bahadur reached the Madore Mahal he found Rabindra waiting for him.

Rabindra had been absent for a week. No one knew where he went, or when he would return from one of his sudden departures from amongst them. No one ever questioned him. He came and went as he chose, but there was always a reason for his mysterious behaviour, and he always brought news of one sort or another.

As soon as Dil Bahadur had dismounted from his horse, Rabindra led him to the seat under the trees. "Dil Bahadur, I must talk to you. Will you listen carefully to what I have to say — it is a matter for haste, once you have heard what I have learned."

He looked tired, and travel worn. He had not even taken time to bathe and change his clothes. "Brother, Jungdah is throwing a shadow over you again. Oh, no don't try to tell me anything — I know that Jamshyd has been deeply hurt — that Yasmin is to marry Sadik

236

Khan — I know all that. But unless we do something about Ismail Mohammed, I think Amara Begum will be fortunate to keep her life — Ismail Mohammed is mad. I have been following him about, listening to him, watching him. He is dangerous for you too. He has certainly discovered that Yasmin is your child. It has turned his brain — you did not know how things were between the two of them Dil Bahadur."

He paused, and Dil Bahadur said, "No. I was a fool. I should have brought her away with me all those years ago — but how is she in danger? He would not harm her, Rabindra. He loves her. He is more likely to murder me."

"Oh yes — he may well try to do that, too. You say you were a fool, Brother. You were only a fool in imagining that Amara Begum and Ismail Mohammed would find happiness in marriage together. How could they, Dil Bahadur? She had given her heart to you. He is naturally a jealous and possessive husband — if she could have felt passion for him, things might have gone better for them — but she was not passionate.

237

She was dutiful, a good, patient wife. He became frustrated and suspicious and jealous. He did not know who she was in love with, but he had enough perception to know that there was someone. Well, he has already sworn publicly that he is going to accuse his wife of adultery before the courts, and before the Panchayat — and now he will name you."

Dil Bahadur had been listening with mounting horror. He could discount anything said to the courts, but the Panchayat — that collection of evil-minded old men — they would turn the story into another stick to beat the ruler with.

"Rabindra, what can I do? The Panchayat will seize with pleasure on any story of that nature."

"That is not so serious. We can prove that you have not seen Amara Begum for sixteen years. You have not been in Jungdah for sixteen years. You left the state two months before Ismail Mohammed's wedding. That can all be proved. A little silver will shut the mouths of anyone in Jungdah. In any case, you are still the great lord who saved the people in Jungdah in their time of need. No one there will smirch your name. But Amara Begum — she is in danger and he will try to kill her one of these days. Do you know, he has been sitting outside Jungdah House every night for a week? There is nowhere for her to go, if he loses the last of his feeble hold on his sanity. It is time he was relieved of his troubled life, Dil Bahadur. There is a Pathan who can shoot the eye out of a peacock . . . "

Dil Bahadur turned to look at his friend of many years. "Do you mean a bought killer Rabindra?"

Rabindra did not reply in words, he looked steadfastly into Dil Bahadur's eyes. Dil Bahadur could not sustain his look. He turned his head away, and sat quietly for a few minutes, thinking. To be rid of this inconvenient and dangerous man — who, by all accounts, must be desperately unhappy. To free Amara Begum from fear, to clear a path . . . His thoughts stopped there.

There was no happiness for him that way. To meet the man in fair fight and kill him, yes — but this was a man who had, in fact, no quarrel with him. They had been friends, brothers in battle. No. Rabindra saw his answer on his face and held up his hand.

"I understand you, Dil Bahadur. But I wish that you felt differently. This man could start a scandal that will affect so many of those nearest to you — Jamshyd, Jiwan Khan — and the marriage so carefully arranged by Amara Begum — imagine what a bad scandal could do to that — have you thought of all this? It would be quick and easy and end trouble."

"No. That is not our way, Rabindra — you know that. But I will go and see him. He used to listen to me before — perhaps he will again. I will try to make him understand that what he thinks is all heated imagination — he must know that I have not seen her, nor been near Jungdah since we drove Sagpurna's troops from the state. I am sure he will listen."

He listened to you before, thought Rabindra, because then he did not think of you as a rival — now he will certainly not listen. But it would do no good to argue with his friend. When Dil Bahadur's mind was made up, there was no moving him. He asked, "If you are going to go and talk to Ismail, choose your time. He is drinking very heavily. I think the best time would be just before sunset. He sleeps the daylight hours away. You know where he is, the Serai — he has a room there. The old Arabserai."

"Yes, so I heard. I will go tomorrow evening, before sunset."

"And I will come with you," said Rabindra, and, having decided already what action he was going to take, did not think that Dil Bahadur would have any trouble with Ismail Mohammed.

★ ★ ★

The long day's excitement and discoveries kept Dil Bahadur awake on his bed. It was midnight when Jamshyd knocked and came in. Dil Bahadur stood up to face him. His son made things clear at once.

"Father. Atlar Khan has told me everything. I know there can be no marriage for me with Yasmin. I know why."

Before Jamshyd's dignified control, Dil Bahadur could not offer a word of apology or explanation. There were no words. He met his son's eyes, and asked him what his plans were. Jamshyd was obviously relieved that there was not to be an emotional scene, or remorseful explanations.

"Jiwan Khan wishes me to finish my time of duty here with him, and then I shall take some leave. I will go down with Atlar Khan to Delhi to stay with Colonel Windrush. He will leave for England, I am told, at the beginning of the month and I will go with him."

That which I greatly feared, thought Dil Bahadur, but did not argue.

"Will you go to Moxton Park and see your mother?"

"No, father. I will not be in England long enough. I am going to take what used to be called 'The Grand Tour' — France, Germany, Italy and Greece. Then from Greece, I come home."

"Home . . . ?"

"Back to the valley of course. Why,

Father, did you think I could leave Lambagh? Never. I only go for this visit because I must. I cannot bear — I could not bear to see her again and turn away as I had to today." The look in his son's eyes twisted Dil Bahadur's heart. He stepped forward and took his son into his arms, and felt no embarrassment over the tears that were on both their faces. Then Jamshyd stepped back, managed a smile for his father and left him.

14

ISMAIL MOHAMMED had finally
sacked the men he had engaged
to watch Dil Bahadur and Amara
Begum. He flung their money at them
and told them to keep away from him
— or it would be the worse for them.
He no longer believed them, he knew
that they were lying when they told him
the same story every evening. He would
do his own watching.

Every night he went down the road
to Jungdah House and either concealed
himself at the big gates, or went round to
the back of the property and watched the
stables. He saw nothing and nobody. The
Begum Roshanara called once and took
his wife and Yasmin out in her carriage,
which was curtained so that he could
not see anything of them. He followed
the carriage and saw them drive into the
palace of the ruler of Dhar, heard the
sounds of music, laughter, and women's
voices and knew that they were attending

a party — they would be in the purdah quarters and no man would be able to approach them there.

After that he took to attending the parties to which he was invited as a matter of course, as a visiting ruler. He had no friends — the few princes he knew well, greeted him with civility and left him alone. He had never been part of their society. He had been a mercenary soldier for too long, hiring himself and his troops out to these princes. It was only when he married Amara, the daughter of the Khan of Jungdah, that he had been recognised as a ruler.

Because he was angered and hurt by his reception, he drank too much. His rage grew and grew with frustration. Dil Bahadur was never at these large feasts — or, as he began to suspect, never at the parties to which *he* was invited. He began to attend parties to which he had not been asked, and drank too much to give him courage. It was hard to be the one who was not included in a conversation. When he joined a group it would soon break up and he would be left standing alone. He was too often rude because his feelings were hurt, and because, even if he was being included in a group, he did not appear to be listening to anything that was said. His sad, wild eyes would be searching the room or the garden, watching other groups, looking for someone — who? Men who had known him before, some, in fact, who had employed him to train their soldiers, or bring in his own to assist in a border dispute, remarked on how changed he was.

The House of Pomegranates became the only place where he felt at ease; he did not realise that the girls were afraid of him, and tried to avoid being engaged by him. The only one he really wanted was the beautiful, popular favourite, Lara. But Lara was in great demand, could afford to pick and choose among her customers, and he was frequently disappointed, and his inner hurt, and his rage against life, fed on his disappointments. Lara began to wear the face of Amara — in those moments when for a minute or two he was able to forget himself, he called her Amara. He had become a haunted man.

* * *

In the House of Pomegranates the lamps were burning brightly, the place was riotous with sound, there was music, laughter and the shouted conversation of men who could not make themselves heard in any other way above the din that roared in the downstairs room. Hazy with smoke from the fumes of the big charcoal stove that was built against one wall, the house was well into its usual overcrowded scene of hilarious enjoyment.

There was an upstairs balcony jutting out over a quarter of the room. Rabindra had a favourite table there, overlooking the whole room, a useful bird's eye view. Tonight he was sitting there, comfortably ensconced on a low cushioned divan, talking to Lara — or rather doing what he always did — saying a few words and asking a few questions, and listening intently to everything that was said, and watching everything that was going on below.

Pretty Lara was glad to be with him. He frequently booked her evenings if she was not going out to dance and otherwise

247

entertain at one of the princely banquets. To be able to sit quietly beside Rabindra, talking to him, listening to what he said, with coffee and brandy on the table in front of them, and her silver hooka to hand as well — and to be *paid* for this — was wonderful to her. She gave Rabindra in return, measure for measure, what he liked most — news and gossip.

Tonight she noticed that Rabindra was quieter than usual, that he seemed to be thinking deeply, and that he was watching the people below as if he was waiting for a particular person.

"You wait for someone, Rabindra?"

"Yes. I wait for Ismail Mohammed."

"Agh — that monster. Is he your friend?"

"No. He is no friend of mine. But tonight I have business with him."

Lara twisted her face into an expression of disgust. "I am sorry for you in that case. He came in earlier this evening. He was already drunk then. He went off somewhere, telling us that he would return, and he spoke as if he imagined we would be glad to see him. If he did not pay so well he would be forbidden the house."

Rabindra poured himself a glass of wine, and gestured to the waiting servant to bring another flask. He was drinking more than he usually did, and Lara noticed it.

"You are disturbed, Rabindra — is it because you have to talk with this man?"

He did not answer her question. He leaned across the table, and looked into her eyes. "Are you my true friend, Lara? I think you are. I need your help tonight. I have a task to perform — I cannot do it without you. What do you say?"

The servant came back then with the fresh flask of wine. She waited until he had gone out of earshot, and then said, "What do you wish me to do for you — is it a great task?"

"No. Not great, and not a long task. Lara, I went to the shop of Janki tonight. I have from her what I needed, and she knows what I will use it for. And look."

He put his hand into the bosom of the loose robe he wore and took out first a package, and then a small flat tin, a snuff box. He pushed the package across to Lara, who took it gingerly.

"Open it Lara, please. I chose the things with care. *They* do not come from Janki. Only the snuff box comes from her."

She opened the package and gasped. "No indeed! These do not come from Janki. Here is a king's ransom."

"Say rather, a queen's ransom. Do you like them?" Lara held up the tasselled gold earrings, and a jewelled comb that dazzled with pearls and rubies.

"Wah! You ask if *I* like them? Did you choose these for me?"

"Who else would I chose them for? The comb for your hair, the earrings for your ears — no one else has such shell-like ears. Put them on and let me see."

While Lara adjusted the comb in her heavy knot of red hair, and hung the earrings in her ears, her green eyes were searching Rabindra's face.

"The help you want from me must be very important. Is it dangerous, this deed you want me to do?"

Rabindra looked and sounded offended.

"Lara! Please. These are gifts to the only intelligent woman I know, who is also beautiful. They have nothing to do with any task. There is of course, payment for the help I ask from you — but that is quite apart from any present I choose to give my beautiful friend."

"Walahi! Your tongue is dipped in honey tonight. My friend, tell me what you would like me to do."

"It is very easy. I want Ismail Mohammed to come up here and sit and drink wine with us for a short time — just long enough for him to drink one glass of this excellent wine. Then I want you to take him to your room, and to bed. You say he pays well — can you endure another hour with him — in your bed? To help me? Is it too difficult?"

Lara was really staring at Rabindra now, frowning, thinking hard. Finally she said, "There is something here I do not understand — but I trust you. I will do it. It is not hard — the hardest part will be mine — in my room. Whatever you plan to pay me, I will have earned it."

"Thank you, my queen. Now we watch

for the coming of Ismail Mohammed — and I promise bangles to match the earrings if we succeed."

"And if we fail?"

"We must not fail — that is the only condition I lay on you — with your charm, we cannot fail if you exert all your wiles."

Presently there was a flurry of arrival in the already crowded room, and Lara looked over the balcony. "Hah! Now I begin to earn my pay. He arrives. I will go down and charm the serpent." She laughed and getting up, ran down the stairs into the room below, where her arrival was greeted by shouts of pleasure as she pushed her way through to where Ismail Mohammed was talking — or rather shouting — at two men.

On the balcony, Rabindra beckoned to the servant, and asked for a dish of ice, and another flask of wine. As soon as the man had gone, Rabindra picked up the little flat box and opened it, and took out one or two pinches of the powder it contained and dropped it into his wine. The tin was back in the pocket in his robe and he was swirling the wine in his glass, and sniffing it with appreciation when Lara, laughing, with her arm supporting Ismail Mohammed, came to the table.

"See the beautiful fish I have caught downstairs — he is my beautiful fish for the evening. Sit, fish, and meet a friend of mine."

Ismail Mohammed swayed himself down among the cushions, it looked unlikely that he would be able to rise. He was staring at Rabindra, and raising his hand he pointed unsteadily at him.

"I have seen you before — I know that face. Have you been to Jungdah? Did you come once — I *know* that face."

Rabindra laughed. "Of course you know my face. I sat opposite you at the Raza banquet — and you spent the evening trying to sell me a horse. Come my friend, you are fuddled with drink — I do not think we need another flask of wine tonight, you will not be able to do justice to your other pleasures — which would be a pity. But this is good wine, brought down over the hills from Kabul vineyards."

Ismail Mohammed was very drunk. He

was also, as always, very argumentative. He stared across at Rabindra, and said, "I am not at all drunk. I can drink more than anyone else in this house. You know that, don't you, girl? You know all about me, and I know all about you — where's this wine you told me about."

Rabindra put his hand out to hold on to his glass.

"I have sent for some fresh wine, Lara — an unopened flask — this last one tasted sour, a little."

"Oh? That is strange — wait, I will go and see what the servant is doing."

But Ismail Mohammed had seen Rabindra's hand grab for his glass, and at once wanted that glass and no other.

"And no waiting. Give me that glass, you — and *you* stay here." He gripped Lara none too gently by her arm, and reached across the table for Rabindra's full glass. He sipped, said, "Nothing wrong with this," and gulped it all down. Rabindra shrugged, and looked ashamed, the expression of a man who had tried to keep his glass of wine to himself. The servant appeared with a fresh flask, and

Ismail Mohammed had a glass of that as well. Then Lara stood up.

"If you wish, you can stay here with your friend and drink the rest of the evening away — or will you come and taste the sweetness of the night with me?"

Ismail Mohammed was stretching across the table to reach the wine flask, and paid her no attention. Lara bit her lip, and looked across at Rabindra. He stood up at once.

"Lara — he is no longer capable of enjoying anything — look at him! Take me to your room, let me taste the sweetness of a night in your company."

He had raised his voice, and Ismail Mohammed suddenly registered what he was saying.

"You thieving son of a pig! Lara is mine for the evening — do you think I pay for you to take your pleasures with her? Get away from her!"

Clutching the flask by the neck he raised it and brought it down in a blow aimed at Rabindra's head. Rabindra dodged and flung himself to one side just in time — The heavy earthenware flask missed his head but even so it hit his shoulder with force enough to bring him to his knees. The flask smashed and wine poured over Rabindra's robe, the table and the cushions of the divan.

Rabindra did not rise. Ismail Mohammed was standing over him with a knife in his hand and murder in his eyes. Lara cried out, and the table servant called, and one of the Pathan watchmen came running, and dragged Ismail back. Lara told the men to take the struggling nawab down to her room.

"Though what he will do there is unknown to me," said Lara as she helped Rabindra to rise. "Are you hurt, my friend?"

"No. Lara, tell me, what happens when one of your patrons has so much to drink that he is incapable and falls down into slumber, and cannot be wakened?"

"Huh! I send for a carriage, he is carried down the back stairs and placed in the carriage and taken back to his home — wherever it is."

"I see. Has this ever happened to Ismail Mohammed?"

"You should ask me how many times

it has happened — it is a weekly habit — sometimes twice a week. I think — I pray — it will be so tonight. There are always two or three Victorias waiting at the back gate for gentlemen who are overcome by their evening's entertainment. No one uses these vehicles more often than the honourable Nawab of Jungdah. I sometimes ask myself what his wife thinks." Rabindra was standing up, trying to wring out his robe.

"His wife lives alone with her daughter. He lives in a room in the old Arab Serai."

The servant had come back and was waiting to be noticed.

"Shankar? What is it? How is the patron?"

"I regret, lady, he is awake and making a disturbance, calling for you."

"Aieeya — I shall have to go. Rabindra, there are clean robes always ready here, and a room and bathroom, if you wish to change and rid yourself of the wine. Shankar will show you. I hope you will allow me to replace the wine and the coffee." She smiled beguilingly at him and said, "You are not in a hurry? I think I will be back very soon, will you wait?"

"I am no longer in a hurry, I will wait, and I will be delighted to wash away the wine and have clean clothes." And, he added to himself, I do not think I will have to wait very long.

He went with Shankar to wash and change, and while doing this he had the opportunity of emptying his snuff box down the bathroom drain.

The balcony was clean and orderly again, there was a fresh flask of the good red wine of Kabul waiting for him. He sat down on clean, dry cushions of purple velvet, thanked Shankar, ordered a jug of fresh coffee for Lara, and prepared to wait patiently for her coming. It was not long before he heard her calling Shankar, and soon after he heard her slippered feet tapping down the stairs, and looked up smiling to greet her.

"He sleeps," said Lara. "He raised his hand to strike me for keeping him waiting, choked and fell down. For a moment I thought he was dead, but he was only asleep. Shankar will put him in a carriage and send him off. Did I do all that you wished? Was everything right?"

She was as calm and cheerful as always, but Rabindra detected anxiety in her eyes.

"Everything is right — you did all I wished, and more, my queen among women."

"Rabindra — you said you went to Janki's shop. What did you buy there?"

"A powder," said Rabindra, "A powder to clear my head and bring sweet sleep."

He smiled at Lara, who was looking puzzled and alarmed.

"A powder for sleep?" she said doubtfully.

"Yes. A powder for long sweet sleep. Have you visited Janki's shop?"

Janki sold more than powders for sleep. Many of the girls visited her. Lara answered him obliquely. "We all know of Janki and her shop."

"Ah. I go there often. A place of marvels. Janki is a friend of mine since I was a young boy. Today, while she mixed my powder, we spoke of the old days, when she owned The House in the Wall, gifted to her by the Lambagh ruler. We spoke of happenings of the past, and old friends, of the old ruler, Kassim Khan, and his son Jiwan Khan, and his adopted son, Dil Bahadur. Janki remembers them all. She took the oath of fealty to the ruler — and kept it faithfully."

"What oath is that?"

"My life for yours, now and always." His voice had changed as he said these words, it sounded as if he was taking the oath himself. His eyes seemed to have become opaque, he was looking at something, some place that she could not imagine. She had always found Rabindra fascinating, and puzzling, a hidden man. Now she began to find him frightening too.

But she forgot the fright when he leaned forward and put a velvet bag in front of her, a bag that was heavy, and made a most satisfactory chinking sound, the sound of good silver coins.

Rabindra stood up to take his leave.

"Lara. You have forgotten everything." He made it a statement, not a question.

"Everything," said Lara hurriedly, the fear coming back into her mind. "I have forgotten everything — there was, after all, nothing to remember — except the gold at my ears, and the jewelled comb in my hair. I will remember them."

He smiled at her then and she watched him walk away, and felt, deep within her, the warning he had not given her. She shivered suddenly, and reached for the wine.

15

YASMIN had slept deeply, a drugged, dream-ridden sleep. When she was awakened by Shanti, the night was just leaving the sky. She lay back on her pillow and watched the darkness begin to lift, the morning star slowly fade as the light brightened — and it was day. The day that was to begin a new life for her, a life for which she had no map, no known path to follow. The month that lay between her and the day of her marriage was like a road leading up hill to unexplored country. She felt fear and great reluctance to face the future; yet underlying these feelings, because she was very young, was a spark of curiosity and mild interest.

They started their journey to Panchghar as soon as they had broken their fast with bread and coffee. They were a small company. Shanti was the only woman servant with them, old Chini

Ayah would follow later with the greater part of the household and their baggage. Travelling with Amara and Yasmin were four mounted guards, a small travelling carriage and horses, two mounted syces leading two spare horses.

Neither Amara Begum nor Yasmin looked back as they rode through the north gate and left the red walls of Madore behind them. They joined the Grand Trunk Road; they would be travelling along it for the first day of their week's journey. It was a good time to leave the city, there were so many people beginning journeys all round them that they travelled unnoticed. In any case, two veiled women and a small entourage would draw little attention — a country Begum returning home after a visit to the great city — that was all that anyone interested enough to do more than glance at them would see.

They made good time in spite of the throngs of travellers who were moving up and down the road. They halted for two hours at noon, when the heat of the day was at its height. Under the dark shade of the trees at the side of the road, well away from the dust clouds of the traffic, Amara and Yasmin threw their veils back, and Shanti brought their food and drink to them before withdrawing to sit with the men.

As they ate and drank, Amara spoke to her daughter for the first time that day.

"Yasmin, is it well with you?"

"I am well, thank you Mother."

"Did you sleep?"

Yasmin's eyes were accusing. "I could do nothing else, mother. Shanti's drug was strong. I slept a strange sleep, full of sorrowful dreams. I cannot remember the dreams now, but I know that all night I was searching for something I had lost."

Her voice was cold, and her use of the word 'Mother' was strange, she normally used the loving diminutive 'Ma-ji'. Would she ever use it again, wondered Amara, or was this coldness of heart towards her going to last for the rest of their lives. She sighed, and Yasmin turned her face away and called to Shanti, asking for her fan. Shanti came to her.

"Your fan — I could not find it,

Yasmin piyari. I thought you had it with you."

Yasmin looked down at her empty hands, remembering then where the fan must be. She could do nothing about the tears that began to overflow her eyes. Shanti was distressed to see her weep, and bent over her. "Child, do not weep for your fan."

"No, Yasmin, do not weep. When we reach Panchghar, we will get another fan for you."

Did they really think that she was weeping for her fan? They were treating her as a child. Anger burned in her. She looked at her mother and said, "I am not a child. I am not weeping for a fan. I weep for something I have lost. The life I would have lived." She spoke so bitterly that Amara was shocked, and could think of nothing to say. They did not speak again, and presently it was time for them to resume their journey.

By sunset they had reached the place where the road that led to the hills branched off from the Grand Trunk Road. This was where they would spend the night. There were other people camping there. Amara led her company further into the trees until they found a small clearing. There they stopped and the horses were unsaddled and unyoked from the carriage, the guards unloaded bedding rolls, and Shanti opened them and spread thick cotton quilts and pillows on the ground. Amara and her silent daughter rested while the guards made a fire, and Shanti began to prepare their evening meal.

★ ★ ★

Twenty miles away, in Madore, the news of Ismail Mohammed's death came to the Madore Mahal.

His servants were used to him returning late into the night, very overtaken with drink. They had learned not to try to rouse him, but to let him sleep on until he called for them. His old bearer, who brought the news to the Madore Mahal was distressed by the news he brought. He had been with Ismail Mohammed for many years, and remembered him as a young, strong man, full of ambition and generous to his servants.

"I waited for his call, but this day it did not come — and when it was late into the afternoon, I went in to wake him, but he did not wake, and I saw that all was not well with him — I sent the chokra for a doctor. The doctor came and said at once that the Nawab was taken by death — that he had been dead for some hours. He did not call to me lord, before he died — I would have heard, I sat all day against his door, and heard nothing. He died in his sleep, the doctor said. I, being distressed, I sent the chokra to tell the news to the Begum Sahiba, but he came back to tell me that the Begum Sahiba had left the house very early, and started for the hills. Then, together, we, his servants, took his body to the Mosque, and he will be carried to the place of the dead before sunset — I being an old man, grown old in his service, am full of sorrow. Will the Jung Sahib, who was his friend, send news of his death to the Begum, his wife, and to his friends?"

Dil Bahadur and Jiwan Khan exchanged a long look. They too remembered Ismail Mohammed, a man of ambition, passionately in love with his Begum, who was now riding into the hills, knowing nothing of what had happened.

They sent messages to all the mountain rulers. The burial would take place that evening. All the time that Dil Bahadur was dealing with the necessary details of the funeral, he was thinking, not of the dead man, but of Amara and her daughter, already started on their long trek to the hills. He rode round to Jungdah House, not trusting the chokra, and found the gates unguarded and the house locked and shuttered, the stables empty. He wondered what escort she had taken for her safety on the journey. This thought sent him to the guard house at the north gate of the city. The men on duty there said that the lady and her daughter had ridden through the gates shortly after sunrise, and that the party had been a small one, four armed men and a woman servant, and a travelling carriage — and baggage ponies. Dil Bahadur went back to the Madore Mahal, spoke to Jiwan Khan, and asked for leave of absence.

"Am I a leper that everyone wants to

leave me? Jamshyd is staying like a dog on a chain, Atlar Khan will leave with him when he goes — Sadik is on leave for his marriage — and now you. How am I supposed to deal with all these princes for the last week of this terrible Durbar."

"I know this is a bad time to ask — but I must go. I must catch up with Amara before she starts on the hill road — she is travelling with no escort to speak of, and also she does not know of her husband's death. I would like to go directly after the burial, with your permission."

"Or without it," said Jiwan Khan, nodding at him. "I know the look in your eyes all too well — and if I say no to you, you will go in any case, which would be undignified for us both. Heh — I wish I could come with you, but alas I am chained by duty. Only one thing I ask. Do not go to Jungdah, brother. As soon as the news of Ismail's death breaks, there will be turmoil there." He stopped speaking, stared at Dil Bahadur, and said, "But that is exactly what you are planning to do — am I right?" Dil Bahadur sighed.

"You read my mind, Jiwan. Yes. I had thought to take Amara to her brother in Panchghar, and then go on from there and keep Jungdah quiet until after the wedding — then she can come and take over the state, while the men in Delhi make up their minds about who is to rule. She is the heir, the daughter of the old ruler — she has a right."

"She is the heir by blood. But a woman inheriting? Of late years I only know of one. Do you think the men in Delhi will agree?"

"If they put it to the vote of the people of Jungdah, they will have to agree. She has been ruling them in all but name for some time, while Ismail Mohammed bred his horses, and trained his army. The people will choose her."

Jiwan Khan looked at him thoughtfully.

"And you will be there to strengthen her arm. Hmm. Are we to lose you, Dil Bahadur? Will you stay among those mountains with her?"

Dil Bahadur met his eyes, and looked away. Then he said quietly,

"Never. I took the oath to your father, and repeated it again to you. My life for yours, now and always. But I think I will spend time there."

Jiwan Khan put his hand on Dil Bahadur's shoulder.

"That is seen, my brother. Take your leave — but come back to us in due course."

★ ★ ★

The sun was setting as they carried Ismail Mohammed's body from the Mosque to the Moslem cemetery, a mile outside the city walls. There were few mourners. Only Dil Bahadur, Jiwan Khan the Ruler of Lambagh, Atlar Khan, and Sadik of Chikor followed the open coffin, taking turns to shoulder it, while two women, paid mourners, wailed and screamed his name, beat their breasts and tore their hair as was suitable and customary. The evening wind had strengthened as the sun went down, and stinging clouds of dust blew about the desolate place. Ismail Mohammed, dressed in his best and wrapped in a clean white sheet, was taken from the coffin and lowered into his grave. The coffin was carried away to be used again. The women stopped mourning and, adjusting their veils, accepted their money and hurried away. Each man stepped forward and threw a handful of earth into the grave, and the grave diggers began their work of covering the grave. The four princes walked out of the cemetery, through the rough gate in the thorn hedge that surrounded it. Jiwan Khan waited for Dil Bahadur and drew him to one side.

"I want you to take a company of your men with you, and be sure that your man Alam Beg is among them. Have a care to yourself, and send word — and do not stay away too long, or I shall myself come looking for you."

"As once before, brother," said Dil Bahadur smiling. The two men embraced, and Jiwan Khan walked away.

Atlar Khan made his farewells and left, but Sadik was still there, waiting in the dusty, waning light. As soon as Dil Bahadur was alone, Sadik came to him.

"Jung Sahib. I heard of your plan. I have a request — allow me to come too. It is my betrothed you will escort. It is fitting that I am part of your company."

Dil Bahadur had known Sadik from birth, his father, the Nawab of Chikor was a close friend, and Sadik's friendship with Jamshyd had brought him into the family. The two young men were the same age. Now this friendship was in danger of being damaged by this unhappy affair of Jamshyd and Yasmin — and the Chikor marriage offer. He presumed that the Chikor family knew nothing of Yasmin's connection to him — if there had been any gossip at the time of his meeting with Amara, they either had not heard it, or, hearing it, had discounted it as being part of the usual gossip that ran through the courts of all the princes — an amusing and totally untrue story. He felt that there was no way that Sadik could not have known about Jamshyd's interest in Yasmin — therefore he had not behaved in a particularly honest way. A word in the ear of his mother to the effect that his friend was interested in the girl would have prevented the offer being made. That word had not been spoken, obviously. But if there had been no offer, how would Amara have prevented her daughter from entertaining serious thoughts of marriage with Jamshyd? It was a terrible coil, thought Dil Bahadur, and knew that it was unfair to blame Sadik, or associate him with Jamshyd's present unhappiness, but it was very difficult not to blame him.

And now, this request that Sadik had made. He longed to refuse it, and knew that in the circumstances he must not. The friendship between Lambagh State and Chikor was of more importance than any personal feelings. Indeed, the vow he had made to the Lambagh family — 'My life for yours, now and always' was a hard one to keep sometimes.

Sadik was waiting for his answer. Dil Bahadur agreed that he should come, and tried to keep his feelings out of his voice. Sadik bowed, and stepped back. If he had noticed Dil Bahadur's hesitancy, he showed no sign. He thanked Dil Bahadur and said, "I would have gone after them myself, but it seems better that we travel together. I have twenty of my men ready to leave with me. When do we go?"

Dil Bahadur found himself approving of the determination in the young man's voice. He had always liked the boy, and now made up his mind that he would not allow any of the present trouble to touch the old friendship.

"We go tonight. If we leave just after moon rise, and ride through the night, we should come up with the Begum's party before they break camp in the morning and begin to go up the hill roads." He remembered well the roughness of those roads, and the desolate plateau they would have to traverse to reach the first of the passes into Panchghar. A difficult journey — that Amara should have risked making it without a proper escort was madness. What had possessed her? He suddenly remembered his last words to her — "I had thought you unchanged . . . but where is your heart?"

He had spoken coldly out of his disappointment that she had refused Jamshyd's offer. Could his cruel words have made her feel she wanted to get away from Madore, lest they should meet again? He felt wildly impatient to be off on the journey, and it was a relief to find that Sadik was as impatient as he was. They agreed to meet at the Madore Mahal and start their journey from there.

Once back in the Madore Mahal, Dil Bahadur sent out orders for a company of the Lambagh Lancers to make ready to accompany him to the hills. Risaldar Major Alam Beg was requested to wait on him immediately in the Madore Mahal. Alam Beg, who had been born in Jungdah, knew routes through the mountain regions to Panchghar and Jungdah. Having made all his arrangements, Dil Bahadur bathed and dressed, and then sent his servant to ask if he could speak with Roshanara Begum, the ruler's wife, before he left. His servant returned to say that Roshanara Begum would be happy to see him. He went at once to the Zenana.

Roshanara was sitting out in her walled court where a fountain played and the air was cool and scented with the flowers of the Jasmine bushes that grew against the walls. Roshanara, lightly dressed in creamy muslins and bare-headed, beckoned him forward and told him to sit on the deep-piled cushions beside her.

"You follow Amara, Jiwan Khan tells me. Does she know you are coming?"

"No. I have not spoken with her for two days — and then the meeting was not happy. Roshanara, tell me why she left so suddenly, without waiting for an escort, or telling anyone her plans — was she running from the possibility of a meeting with me?"

Roshanara sighed. "I do not know. She sent me no message. She was angered with me a little, I think. I told her that I thought it was unwise of her to attend this Durbar — with her heart still turning to you in spite of all the years that have passed. I was afraid that it would cause pain for her, and perhaps bad trouble with Ismail Mohammed. But then, at the Dhar banquet I saw where the pain — and the trouble — was going to strike." She paused and looked at Dil Bahadur. He was silent, startled that she should speak so openly of Amara's love for him. He had accepted long ago that the two women were close in loving friendship, as well as being cousins, that Roshanara must know everything about the love affair that had run through their lives. But there had never been a whisper from her till now.

Roshanara knew she had shocked him, but she continued steadily, "Yes. At the Dhar banquet I saw Yasmin's eyes as she looked down through the trellis of the Purdah balcony, while Jamshyd looked up as if his eyes could pierce the screen and see her. I was afraid for them then. It is too late to say it now, but I will. Why did you not take Amara then to be your second wife? You had the right."

"I am only a man. I could not see the future. I could only do what I thought was right."

His voice was so full of sadness that Roshanara's eyes filled with tears. "Ah, Dil Bahadur. Love is cruel."

"It is indeed — and through me, so many have suffered. Even, I fear, Ismail Mohammed — if he guessed."

"Yes. I think myself he knew. He looked like a man tormented. Dil Bahadur — have you seen Yasmin?"

"Not yet. Is she like her mother?"

"No. I tell you now why I think Ismail Mohammed must have guessed about her. You know the portrait that is in the Diwan-i-am in the palace in Lambagh?"

"The portrait of my mother Muna?"

"Yes. Yasmin is her mirror image. Not yet in full bloom, but that is who she will resemble. And Ismail Mohammed watched her grow — his only child. The child of the woman he adored. He must have known."

Dil Bahadur was silent, almost a silence of despair. He had, in sorrow, returned in his mind to the time when he first met Ismail Mohammed. He saw the man, his eyes glowing with love and passion as he looked at Amara, heard the tones of his voice as he spoke to her. Dil Bahadur tried to find comfort in the fact that from the time Ismail Mohammed showed his love for Amara, he had not gone to her in love. He had said farewell to her, had avoided seeing her again, and had left Jungdah and never returned. But still he felt guilt which would not leave him. He said bitterly, "I was a fool — a blind fool, so afraid of causing pain that I wounded everyone."

Roshanara dried her eyes. "The past is over, Dil Bahadur, and there is nothing we can do there. Those were bad and difficult times for us all." The voice of

279

the fountain filled the silence as they sat together, lost in memories of their days in Jungdah. Horses, blowing and stamping on the drive outside, brought Dil Bahadur to his feet.

"I must go. Roshanara, God keep you in his hand — and Jiwan Khan with you. I have said my farewells to him."

"Wait, Dil Bahadur, brother of my heart. You say you were a fool in those years. Indeed that is true. But what is in your mind for the future? For Amara and for yourself?"

"How can I say — the future is closed to me." He saw the disappointment bitter in her eyes, and said quickly, "Ah Roshanara! Do not be angered with me! If I tell you that I think of Amara constantly, that she torments my sleep and speaks in my ear when I should be thinking of other things — will that be the beginning of an answer to your question?" Her lovely smile lightened her face and she gave him her hand to kiss in farewell.

"Go with God, Dil Bahadur."

Hurrying out to the front of the palace, Dil Bahadur was stopped dead by the sight of his son standing at Sadik Khan's stirrup. Neither of the young men was smiling, nor did they look particularly at ease, but at least there was no sign of the pain and anger he had seen in Jamshyd's eyes the last time he had spoken with him. He decided to stay where he was, in the shadows, and watch and listen. Sadik's men were drawn up behind him, all mounted on good horses, with baggage ponies behind. Sadik tossed a command over his shoulder, and dismounting, gave his reins to the syce who ran up to take his horse. He stood facing Jamshyd, and said quietly, "What you have to say — *if* it is necessary for you to say anything on this subject, say quickly, for your father will be here shortly Jamshyd Khan."

"It is necessary for me to speak with you. Sadik, we have been friends all our lives; never did I imagine that we would speak to each other without friendship."

"Indeed, nor did I. Is this all you wished to say?"

"*No!* Listen to me. I have done Yasmin harm."

"What!" Seeing Sadik's hand fall to his sword hilt, Dil Bahadur started forward,

281

but Jamshyd's next words, and his raised voice halted him.

"Sadik! Stop, you fool, you'll have your men attacking me! How can you think that I would do what you imagine to your affianced bride." His voice dropped lower. "Or to my sister?"

Sadik's sword stayed in its scabbard as in astonishment he repeated, "To your sister?"

"Yes. Yasmin is my sister. Do you think I would have allowed you to take her from me so easily if I had not discovered this?"

Sadik's voice was cold as he said, "Why do you tell me this? I do not need to know — and it will not make the smallest difference."

"I did not imagine it would. I tell you this because I did harm to Yasmin's feelings. I could not, at that time of shocked sorrow, explain to her why we could not marry. I let her think that it was because I myself did not love her — God help me."

There was silence between them, then Sadik said, his voice not so gentle, "Do you also tell me this so that I understand that you were her first love?"

"Do you know me at all — *friend*? I tell you this because I hurt her — let her think she was scorned when she came to me."

"I do not wish to hear what happened between you. It is enough for me to remember you as I have always known you. Any hurt that has been done to Yasmin's heart *I* will heal — without your assistance Jamshyd." He paused, and then held out his hand. "I know you well, *friend*. In a little time perhaps we will be as we were — perhaps?"

Jamshyd did not hesitate. He put his hand into Sadik's hand saying, "Time will pass, and we will change. Sadik, I have something here that Yasmin values — her fan." He put the fan into Sadik's hand, and turning, mounted his horse and rode away past the watching soldiers of Chikor.

16

DIL BAHADUR and Sadik Khan rode together, well ahead of the dust cloud their men raised. The men rode silent and sleepy behind them, with Alam Beg riding ahead of them, keeping them back from the two leaders. At this time of night there was little traffic on the roads and they were able to ride fast, keeping their eyes open for bullock carts. These carts, creaking along at a slow pace were a danger. They were supposed to keep well to the side of the road, but this did not always happen. The drivers slept, and the bullocks drawing the heavily-laden carts chose their own way, and filled the road.

At one of the halts caused by these obstructions, Dil Bahadur, waiting impatiently while his men cleared the road, was joined by Sadik.

"Jung Sahib. I would ask you something."

Dil Bahadur had been expecting this. He wished with all his heart that his son had spoken with him before suddenly telling Sadik about Yasmin's paternity. God knows what he had thought he was doing — Dil Bahadur supposed that it was to ensure that Sadik was patient with a girl who had been, in her own eyes, rejected by the man she loved. But what a risk to run! Sadik could have decided to withdraw from the marriage, and where would that have left Yasmin! Of course, Sadik now had questions to ask — but this was no place to have a private conversation, the middle of the Grand Trunk Road, with a milling crowd of roaring soldiers, overwrought horses and disturbed bullocks surrounding them. He reined his horse back and walked it to the side of the road.

"Sadik, this is no place to talk. Let us wait for a more peaceful halt."

Sadik's voice was tense and to Dil Bahadur's surprise and annoyance, he persisted. "I need the answer to one question — there have been too many rumours. Please, tell me, is Yasmin your daughter?"

Annoyed, Dil Bahadur gave his answer in one short word. "Yes."

There was no opportunity for Sadik to ask any more questions. The long line of carts had been pushed to the side, the road was clear. Dil Bahadur spurred ahead, followed by Sadik.

They came within two miles of their destination, and Dil Bahadur halted the men and ordered them to make camp there.

"We do not want to arrive with a company of mounted, armed men without warning, and frighten the Begum. We could be mistaken for a band of dacoits instead of an escort," he told Sadik. They left the men and went forward together, taking Risaldar Alam Beg with them. They reached the spot where the hill road branched off just before dawn, and dismounting, sat down to wait for the first signs of activity in the Begum's camp.

The sky was lightening, the old fort that gave the place its name, the Purana Kila, was already turning a rose colour in the spreading light and the river showed white through the trees that grew along the banks. There were people sleeping all about the place, but the Begum had taken her party through the trees and was settled on the river bank, with a part of the ruined sandstone wall adding to her privacy. Alam Beg looked towards the Begum's camp and nodded approvingly.

"This spot is well chosen. Amara Begum is a woman of great good sense. Also the guards are well trained, awake and watchful. I go forward, lord, to tell them who we are, lest we get a bullet as a greeting. I will take the horses."

Now that he was so close, within minutes, perhaps, of seeing Amara, Dil Bahadur could think of nothing but this meeting. He hoped that his sudden arrival would not alarm her, and that she would be glad that he had come — that his last hurtful words would be forgiven. His blood rose at the thought of her coming into his arms, and then, like a dash of cold water, he remembered another reason why he was here — to tell her that she was a widow.

Sadik, seated beside him, would have liked to speak with him, but he saw that the man was so withdrawn, so

287

deep in some unhappy thought, that he did not care to disturb him. Instead he sat silent and let his own thoughts wander to his meeting with Yasmin. He felt his heart quicken and lift at the thought of seeing her. He remembered her tears, and the lost expression in her eyes as she raised them to him at their last meeting, and vowed to himself that soon she would shed no more tears over Jamshyd, that she would begin to feel this same excitement that he felt — excitement and pleasure at the thought of their life together.

The light broadened, it was morning. A woman, cloaked and veiled in a white burka crossed the clearing in front of them and walked down towards the river. Dil Bahadur watched her idly, and then realised who he was watching. Even the enveloping burka could not disguise that figure, that poised walk. He looked sidelong at Sadik and saw that he had fallen asleep. Dil Bahadur rose silently to his feet and walked away, following the white robed figure of Amara.

When he caught up with her, she was standing looking down at the water, her veil thrown back from her face. Here the river had narrowed, and the water foamed through its banks, noisy over rocks. She had not heard him approach, and started when he came to stand beside her. She looked at him, amazed and unbelieving. He saw her mouth form his name, but could hear nothing, the voice of the river was so loud. He found her hand in the folds of the burka and led her further along the bank and back into the shelter of the trees.

Time stopped for them. They stood together, looking at each other, unable to speak, her hand still clasped in his. He ached to take her into his arms, but the message he had to give her stood between them like a sword. He let her hand go, and stepped back. She could not understand why he had not embraced her, why she was not held safely against his heart. He looked at her with love, she could see it plainly — something was holding him back. She had a sudden terrible fear that she knew what it was. The English woman. She must be returning — she had stretched out her white hand from that cold place so far away, and had drawn him back. Once more. I have lost him, thought Amara, and did not know how to bear it.

"Amara — I regret, I bring news that will distress you." He saw her brace herself, her brows drew together and her eyes were afraid. He said quickly, "Ismail Mohammed died yesterday. He was buried last night. I have ridden through the night to tell you this."

He saw a shade of relief on her face. She asked, "What happened? Did he fall from his horse?" She had thought it had been an accident. Then she said, "He drinks too much. The Hakim in Jungdah warned him last year."

"The Hakim was right to warn him. He had spent the evening drinking in the House of Pomegranates. It was a very hot night. He died in his sleep, and the doctor who was called said that excess of alcohol had caused him to have a seizure."

She was silent. Was she remembering, as he was, the man Ismail Mohammed had been, ambitious, ardent in love, brave in the face of danger? He could not tell her thoughts. She put up her hand to draw her veil down over her face and he saw that her hand was trembling. It was a gesture of mourning, as if she withdrew herself from the world to hide her sorrow. He could not see her face and he was glad. To see her weep and be unable to give her the comfort of his arms would be unbearable. She walked a few steps away from him and stood with her back turned, and he asked if he should leave her. "I can send your woman."

All she could think was that she wanted to weep in his arms for what her life had been. Regret was bitter in her heart, the wastage of the years appalled her suddenly and she sobbed aloud. Dil Bahadur clenched his teeth at the sound of that bitter weeping. He could not bear it. He stepped forward and took her into his arms. He stood holding her while she wept, and she knew even in her sorrow that he would misinterpret her tears, and raising her head from his shoulder said, "I weep for what I never gave him, because it was all given to you. Everything I am, everything, since I was that child in the garden, everything has been yours. You had better know this, Dil Bahadur, let there be no falseness between us. I cannot mourn him as a wife should, but for his honour's sake I will mourn him as is right, for the customary period. At the end of the month, my life will be my own. It will be the time of the marriage of Yasmin, and no mourning must change, or touch that."

"Yasmin. Our daughter." He felt her stiffen in his arms.

"Who told you that? Atlar Khan?"

"No. I was thinking of you and your refusal to allow a marriage between Jamshyd and Yasmin. I thought as I often do, of the days in Jungdah, and how it would have been if I had taken you for my second wife. Jamshyd would not have had the pain of his love for Yasmin, because had we been married, she would have been my child, and suddenly, I knew, without any doubt, that she was indeed my child. And then I knew what I had done, that I had left you alone, carrying my child — left you when you needed me. I do not know how to bear the pain of my guilt over that. Forgive me, Amara?"

"Forgive you? For what? You only did what you thought was right."

"Ah God! Hell has burst its gates, the devil has found reason for mirth, and wars have swept the earth because men do what they think is right. I was a fool, Amara, you offered me love and happiness and I turned away from you. I beg forgiveness."

"I too did what I thought was right, and married Ismail Mohammed. I think the devil laughed then as well. It is over gone. Let no part of the past touch us now."

It was as if they had buried Ismail Mohammed once more, and the thought of him blew away on the morning wind. The fingers of the past released them. Dil Bahadur tightened his arms round her.

"There is so little time left, after so long apart! I am leaving you in Panchghar, and then I go on to Jungdah and hold the place quiet until you come. What happens after that I know not, but we will meet it together. This is our last parting, Amara. Lift your veil, let me look on your face once again before we have to part." She lifted her hands and threw her veil back. They looked at each other in the bright morning light, and did not see the marks of time and sorrow on each other's faces. They saw what they most longed to see, the face of the beloved.

The camp was awake. Voices called, smoke curled up from newly-kindled fires. It was time to go back to the others, and start their journey to the mountains.

★ ★ ★

Sadik, lying alone where Dil Bahadur had left him, woke with the sun dazzling on his face. He could not think where he was for a moment, then memory came back and he stood up, brushing dust and dry grass from his clothes and trying to shake off the drowsiness that his deep sleep had left with him.

He had been dreaming of Yasmin. She had floated through his dreams like a wraith, her face always turned away from him. He felt a great urgency to find her, talk to her, make her look at him. He set off, walking through the clusters of people packing up to continue their journey, until he reached the ruined wall where the Begum's camp had been set up. He saw Dil Bahadur talking to Alam Beg, and beyond them he saw a splash of colour and walked towards it, and there was Yasmin, sitting watching her woman build a fire and feed it with twigs.

Yasmin was wearing the costume of the people of Jungdah. A wide sleeved crimson robe was belted tightly round her waist, over long, close fitting trousers. On her feet were boots of scarlet leather. She was bare-headed, with no veil, sitting there in the early sunlight, her hands folded in her lap. Her long plait was tied with a scarlet cord, tasselled at the end with turquoises. She was so beautiful that everything Sadik had been going to say flew out of his head.

Yasmin was sitting at peace with herself. Deep in the night, as she lay sleepless and miserable, her mother had come to sit beside her.

"Yasmin. What passed between you and Jamshyd? What is it that has wounded you so badly that you are unable to throw me a civil word. What did he say to make you hate me?"

"Ma-ji — I do not hate you. He said nothing. Nothing at all. I asked him, because I loved him and thought he loved me, to let me be his second wife. Ma-ji, he turned away from me, he said nothing. I am ashamed before you."

Amara heard the pain in the quiet voice. This is my fault, she thought, I should have told her the truth. She took the cold hand Yasmin held out to her, and said, "There is nothing here for shame, Yasmin. Love cannot be ashamed."

"If you offer it, unasked, and it is not returned? I feel of no worth. I am too young, too foolish."

"Yasmin, you are surrounded by love. Do not despise your youth. You are young and beautiful and greatly beloved."

"Yes, by you, my mother, of course I am loved, and thought beautiful."

"You are also loved by your future husband."

"Sadik Khan? How can he love me,

he does not know me."

"That is true — but remember, he chose you. He asked for you, told his mother, it was you or no one."

Yasmin said bitterly, "So did Jamshyd Khan choose me — I thought. But from one minute to the next, he changed. What is to stop Sadik changing his mind? What becomes of me if he changes his mind after marriage? Do I become a widow, will they break my bracelets, shave my head and dress me in white kuddah?"

Now I shall have to tell her the truth thought Amara, and prayed that it was not too late.

"My child, will you listen to me without growing angry? Feel pity for Jamshyd, he did not know how to tell you the truth. Yasmin, Jamshyd Khan, the son of the Jung Sahib Dil Bahadur, is your full brother. His father is your father."

Yasmin stared at her as if she had suddenly gone mad.

"What are you saying, Ma-ji? How can this be?" Amara told her the story of her long love for Dil Bahadur, going back to their first meeting, keeping nothing from her, and Yasmin listened. She listened as if she was listening to a romance being read to her from an old book. As if one of the stories in the book had come to life in front of her. Her mother became the princess in terrible danger. Dil Bahadur the handsome daring prince who rescued her. At the end, when Amara was silent, Yasmin sighed deeply, and said, "Oh Ma-ji, why did you not marry Dil Bahadur? Why did you take Ismail Mohammed for your husband?"

Amara, wise suddenly, stretched the truth a little. "Dil Bahadur was married to the English Begum and had a son — Jamshyd. I would have been a second wife to the English woman, and my father, the Khan of Jungdah would not agree to that. So, you understand Yasmin. You are not the only person who cannot marry the one you think you want."

"Alas, Ma-ji, it is very sad." She said nothing then for a little while, and then, her voice very soft she asked, "Did you love him very much, Ma-ji?"

"Yes. With all my heart."

"Oh alas. How terrible for you — love

298

is very hard, my mother. I feel great sorrow for you."

In her sorrow for me, thought Amara, she has forgotten herself — perhaps? But presently Yasmin said wonderingly, "Jamshyd is my brother. How strange that seems — but it no longer hurts me to think of him. I tell myself now that I have two brothers."

"Yes. And soon, very soon, you will come to feel for Jamshyd the affection that you feel for Atlar Khan. Very soon, there will be another image in your heart — I promise you this."

"In a month — or a week — or a day, I will forget the pain of love? You promise me this?"

"I promise you this. You will forget. Now, will you sleep my daughter?"

Yasmin said softly, "Someone else made me that promise — yes, my mother, I will sleep."

The soft voices died away, and the camp was held in silence.

Now, in the bright morning, with the day beginning all round her, Yasmin, still half in dreams, looked up and saw Sadik. She was young and inexperienced but the

299

look on his face was one she understood at once. She looked away quickly, colour flooding her face. He stopped an arms length away.

"Chandni — I do not have any words. You have taken them all away. You are, all by yourself, a garden of roses." He saw her brows contract a little, heard his own words sounding in his ears, and cursed himself. Fool! Of all the things to say — that damned ruin, the Pila Ghar. The garden there, where she had walked. He said quickly, "I promise you a garden."

"And a lake? For me to sit beside, with Zurah?" So she had seen him that day. He smiled at her.

"Yes. You may sit and watch the birds on the lake, and the lotus floating amongst its leaves. But I shall sit beside you. Not Zurah. Yasmin, stay where you are for one small minute — I have something you value."

She watched him walk away from her, a young man in a great hurry, and thought to herself, I will stay. I will forget about a garden where I will never walk. There will be other gardens . . .

He had returned. He bent and put into her empty hands the peacock fan. The silver handle, the emerald and the blue of the feathers dazzled in her eyes for a moment. Only a moment. Then she looked up and smiled at him.

"Sit with me, nawabzaida Sahib. Sit and talk to me of the lake and the birds, and the pink lotus flowers . . . "

17

WHEN the Durbar in Madore was over, Jiwan Khan, before he left for Lambagh, gave Jamshyd leave.

Jamshyd went climbing up in the heights of Manamahesh and Barra Dhari, on the borders of Lambagh, Sarkhara and Johindi. The giant ranges of the Himalayas received him, the silence of the snows began to heal his heart. At first, the memory of Yasmin was with him every foot of the way. He heard her voice in the long nights, in the sigh of the night winds. The words she had said when he had kissed her — the first time, the only time he had kissed her. The question she had asked sounded in his heart: "Do such kisses mean love?"

After a while her voice faded, she did not walk with him so often. He made himself forget her, and found peace.

One night, sitting beside his camp fire in a valley that lay below the great swell of the Barra Dhari pass, he knew he was ready for civilization again. Atlar Khan was waiting for him to return. Together they would leave for Delhi.

He arrived down on the borders of Pakodi State ten days later, just before sunset. He settled himself in to the old Circuit House on the Khaksar road. That was the rendezvous, Atlar Khan would be coming after sunset, or thereabouts.

He had forgotten the wedding until he saw a crowd of villagers, all in their best clothes, making their way up the steep winding path to Pakodi. The wedding — this must have been the day.

He went out into the garden of the Circuit House and looked over towards the distant white walls of Pakodi Fort. The wind had changed and now he could hear the high call of horns and the deep throbbing, steady as a heartbeat, of the drums. The ceremony must be over, now the dancing girls and the musicians were, no doubt, entertaining the guests.

He stood looking at the fort while shadows streaked the sky and darkness came down like chiffon veils over the scarlet and gold of the sunset. The darkness round him deepened. He waited until he heard Atlar Khan arriving. He had something to do at last — he could go and meet him.

The night wind had strengthened and a rain of white blossoms fell from the creeper over the veranda arches. He put out his hand and caught one and looked down at it. The faint scent, reminding, came to him. Jasmine — flower of the heart.

Atlar Khan was calling his name. It was time to go. He turned away from the lights and the distant music and went to join his friend.

THE END

FATAL RING OF LIGHT
Helen Eastwood

Katy's brother was supposed to have died in 1897 but a scrawled note in his handwriting showed July 1899. What had happened to him in those two years? Katy was determined to help him.

NIGHT ACTION
Alan Evans

Captain David Brent sails at dead of night to the German occupied Normandy town of St. Jean on a mission which will stretch loyalty and ingenuity to its limits, and beyond.

A MURDER TOO MANY
Elizabeth Ferrars

Many, including the murdered man's widow, believed the wrong man had been convicted. The further murder of a key witness in the earlier case convinced Basnett that the seemingly unrelated deaths were linked.

THE WILDERNESS WALK
Sheila Bishop

Stifling unpleasant memories of a misbegotten romance in Cleave with Lord Francis Aubrey, Lavinia goes on holiday there with her sister. The two women are thrust into a romantic intrigue involving none other than Lord Francis.

THE RELUCTANT GUEST
Rosalind Brett

Ann Calvert went to spend a month on a South African farm with Theo Borland and his sister. They both proved to be different from her first idea of them, and there was Storr Peterson — the most disturbing man she had ever met.

ONE ENCHANTED SUMMER
Anne Tedlock Brooks

A tale of mystery and romance and a girl who found both during one enchanted summer.

CLOUD OVER MALVERTON
Nancy Buckingham

Dulcie soon realises that something is seriously wrong at Malverton, and when violence strikes she is horrified to find herself under suspicion of murder.

AFTER THOUGHTS
Max Bygraves

The Cockney entertainer tells stories of his East End childhood, of his RAF days, and his post-war showbusiness successes and friendships with fellow comedians.

MOONLIGHT
AND MARCH ROSES
D. Y. Cameron

Lynn's search to trace a missing girl takes her to Spain, where she meets Clive Hendon. While untangling the situation, she untangles her emotions and decides on her own future.

NURSE ALICE IN LOVE
Theresa Charles

Accepting the post of nurse to little Fernie Sherrod, Alice Everton could not guess at the romance, suspense and danger which lay ahead at the Sherrod's isolated estate.

POIROT INVESTIGATES
Agatha Christie

Two things bind these eleven stories together — the brilliance and uncanny skill of the diminutive Belgian detective, and the stupidity of his Watson-like partner, Captain Hastings.

LET LOOSE THE TIGERS
Josephine Cox

Queenie promised to find the long-lost son of the frail, elderly murderess, Hannah Jason. But her enquiries threatened to unlock the cage where crucial secrets had long been held captive.

THE TWILIGHT MAN
Frank Gruber

Jim Rand lives alone in the California desert awaiting death. Into his hermit existence comes a teenage girl who blows both his past and his brief future wide open.

DOG IN THE DARK
Gerald Hammond

Jim Cunningham breeds and trains gun dogs, and his antagonism towards the devotees of show spaniels earns him many enemies. So when one of them is found murdered, the police are on his doorstep within hours.

THE RED KNIGHT
Geoffrey Moxon

When he finds himself a pawn on the chessboard of international espionage with his family in constant danger, Guy Trent becomes embroiled in moves and countermoves which may mean life or death for Western scientists.

TIGER TIGER
Frank Ryan

A young man involved in drugs is found murdered. This is the first event which will draw Detective Inspector Sandy Woodings into a whirlpool of murder and deceit.

CAROLINE MINUSCULE
Andrew Taylor

Caroline Minuscule, a medieval script, is the first clue to the whereabouts of a cache of diamonds. The search becomes a deadly kind of fairy story in which several murders have an other-worldly quality.

LONG CHAIN OF DEATH
Sarah Wolf

During the Second World War four American teenagers from the same town join the Army together. Forty-two years later, the son of one of the soldiers realises that someone is systematically wiping out the families of the four men.

THE LISTERDALE MYSTERY
Agatha Christie

Twelve short stories ranging from the light-hearted to the macabre, diverse mysteries ingeniously and plausibly contrived and convincingly unravelled.

TO BE LOVED
Lynne Collins

Andrew married the woman he had always loved despite the knowledge that Sarah married him for reasons of her own. So much heartache could have been avoided if only he had known how vital it was to be loved.

ACCUSED NURSE
Jane Converse

Paula found herself accused of a crime which could cost her her job, her nurse's reputation, and even the man she loved, unless the truth came to light.

BUTTERFLY MONTANE
Dorothy Cork

Parma had come to New Guinea to marry Alec Rivers, but she found him completely disinterested and that overbearing Pierce Adams getting entirely the wrong idea about her.

HONOURABLE FRIENDS
Janet Daley

Priscilla Burford is happily married when she meets Junior Environment Minister Alistair Thurston. Inevitably, sexual obsession and political necessity collide.

WANDERING MINSTRELS
Mary Delorme

Stella Wade's career as a concert pianist might have been ruined by the rudeness of a famous conductor, so it seemed to her agent and benefactor. Even Sir Nicholas fails to see the possibilities when John Tallis falls deeply in love with Stella.

CHATEAU OF FLOWERS
Margaret Rome

Alain, Comte de Treville needed a wife to look after him, and Fleur went into marriage on a business basis only, hoping that eventually he would come to trust and care for her.

CRISS-CROSS
Alan Scholefield

As her ex-husband had succeeded in kidnapping their young daughter once, Jane was determined to take her safely back to England. But all too soon Jane is caught up in a new web of intrigue.

DEAD BY MORNING
Dorothy Simpson

Leo Martindale's body was discovered outside the gates of his ancestral home. Is it, as Inspector Thanet begins to suspect, murder?

LARGE PRINT
Gordon, Katharine.
The peacock fan

	DATE DUE	